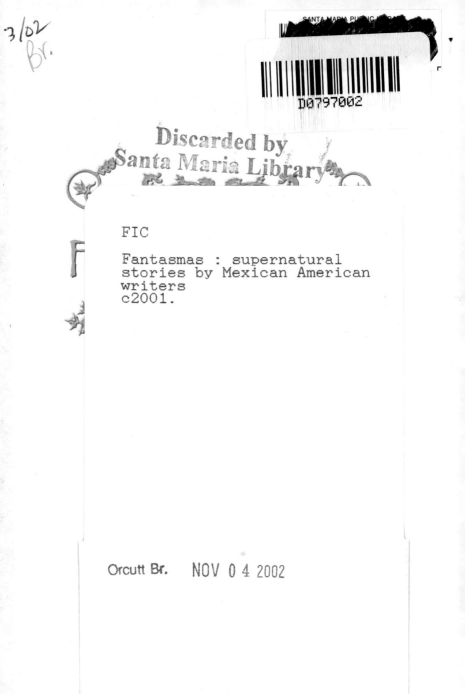

FIC

Fantasmas : supernatural
stories by Mexican American
writers
c2001.

Bilingual Press/Editorial Bilingüe

General Editor
  Gary D. Keller

Managing Editor
  Karen S. Van Hooft

Associate Editors
  Barbara H. Firoozye
  Thea S. Kuticka

Assistant Editor
  Linda St. George Thurston

Editorial Consultant
  Shawn L. England

Editorial Board
  Juan Goytisolo
  Francisco Jiménez
  Eduardo Rivera
  Mario Vargas Llosa

Address:
  Bilingual Press
  Hispanic Research Center
  Arizona State University
  P.O. Box 872702
  Tempe, Arizona 85287-2702
  (480) 965-3867

FANTASMAS

Supernatural Stories
by Mexican American Writers

EDITED BY
Rob Johnson

INTRODUCTION BY
Katheen Alcalá

Bilingual Press/Editorial Bilingüe
Tempe, Arizona

ISBN 1-931010-02-1

Library of Congress Cataloging-in-Publication Data

Fantasmas : supernatural stories by Mexican American writers / edited by Rob Johnson ; introduction by Kathleen Alcalá.
     p. cm.
   ISBN 1-931010-02-1 (alk. paper)
     1. Fantasy fiction, American.   2. Short stories, American—Mexican American authors.
   3. Supernatural—Fiction.   I. Johnson, Rob, 1961-

PS648.F3 F344 2001
813'.087660886872—dc21   2001025282

PRINTED IN THE UNITED STATES OF AMERICA

Cover art: Spectre (2000), *by Quintín González*

Cover and interior design by John Wincek, Aerocraft Charter Art Service

Acknowledgment

"The Plumed Serpent of Los Angeles" was previously published by the *SouthernCross Review* (online journal), number 2, November-December 1999.

CONTENTS

FOREWORD

Rob Johnson

The idea for *Fantasmas* was inspired by a creative writing class I taught at The University of Texas-Pan American in the fall of 1996. I was new to the Rio Grande Valley and was just beginning to discover the richness of border culture. In one assignment for the class, I asked students to take a folktale and retell it as a contemporary short story. As an example, I gave them Native American writer Leslie Marmon Silko's story "Yellow Woman," which is based on Laguna Pueblo legend. The students needed no prompting. Growing up along the border in families whose connections to the motherland of Mexico go back many generations, they had innumerable stories to tell me of *la llorona, la lechuza, el diablo,* and *los espíritus.* Two of the stories written for that class appear in this volume, Rubén Degollado's "Our Story Frays," which mixes Catholicism and curses *(hechizos),* and Stephanie R. Reyes's devil and rancho-revenge tale, "Bad Debts and Vindictive Women."

As an anthologist and editor conditioned to classify literary works, I wondered what "type" of story I was looking at. Were these typical ghost stories and urban legends that every region featured, or were they a specific kind of typical writing? On weekends, I drove from my home in deep, south Texas seven hours up to Austin to do research at The University of Texas's Benson Latin American Collection, one of the key centers for research on writers of the Americas. There, I read numerous examples of supernatural stories by Mexican American writers such as Carmen Tafolla, Pat Mora, Aristeo Brito, and Rudolfo A. Anaya, and I was able to distinguish the origins and characteristics of these stories from those by the more famous Latin American "magical realists," such as Jorge Luis Borges, Gabriel García Márquez, and Julio Cortázar. (In her introduction to this book, Kathleen Alcalá makes this distinction clear.) The term I found that best captured this type of story was one that appeared occasionally in short-story indexes, that of the "cuento de fantasma." Literally translated, this means a "phantom" or "ghost" story, but I found that the label was more generally applied to any story dealing with fantastic or supernatural events. As Kathleen Alcalá points out, in Mexico they are a kind of "pulp" fiction that combines folktales, legend, and pop culture.

For *Fantasmas: Supernatural Tales by Mexican American Writers*, I distributed the following advertisement soliciting original short stories of this type from Mexican American writers: "Written in the spirit of the *cuento de fantasma*, the stories should include some element of folklore, superstition, religion, myth, or history. This supernatural element may be subtle or it may be prominent in the story. I am not looking for simple retellings of folktales or ghost stories, but I am interested in reinterpretations of such tales, particularly if they are placed in a contemporary setting." In other words, I was not proposing to collect folktales but to gather new, imaginative short stories.

The manuscript before you, featuring nineteen stories (most previously unpublished) by both well-known and emerging Mexican American writers, is the result of this solicitation. I believe it captures the spirit of the *cuento de fantasma* in many obvious ways, but also in subtle ways. For example, only one story even mentions the most familiar of border legends, that of the weeping woman, la llorona. Some stories have a slight element of the supernatural informing them, while others are outright ghost stories and fantasies. The stories in *Fantasmas* mirror their Mexican counterparts in that they too are inspired by a variety of influences. The fact that many of the stories are set on the border is appropriate for a literature that moves freely from the high to the low, from reality to the supernatural, from the old world to the new.

Several short stories particularly exemplify my original vision of the book, one that mixes fictional genres, conventions, and the individual vision of Mexican American writers. In "Cantinflas," Stephen D. Gutiérrez tells the story of a young boy terrorized by a puppet he buys at the market on Los Angeles's Olvera Street. Demon dolls are a familiar convention of horror literature, but the story takes on a new life when the doll is a beloved Mexican comic. When I first read "Cantinflas," it struck me as being exactly the mixture of elements that defined *Fantasmas.* Another story, "Beyond Eternity," also excited me for the same reason. Here, I thought, is a brand new mixture of romance (middle-aged romance even!), rancho tale, and traditional ghost story. David Rice's "The Devil in the Valley" also captures an essential element of the book for me. In the story, a young woman asks her grandmother to tell her the story of the devil burning down the church in Edcouch, Texas, in 1953, and the grandmother does, but mostly the story concerns her days working as a *peón* in the canning factories of south Texas. The story thus demonstrates the subterranean political moral of the modern-day *cuento de fantasma:* never forget there is a spiritual side of life, but even more importantly, don't ignore social reality.

David Rice's story was one of the first I received in response to my advertisement, and it was only after I had the manuscript mostly collected that I realized that the issue his story raises is central to understanding the place of these supernatural stories in Mexican American literature. Certainly, Mexican American fiction of the past has more often been noted for its social realism, as opposed to the quality of fantasy and supernaturalism featured in the stories here. A comparison of "Maldición" in *Fantasmas* with the the seminal Chicano novel . . . *y no se lo tragó la tierra/And the Earth Did Not Devour Him* (1971) makes this contrast clear. In "Maldición," the earth opens up to swallow a disrespectful daughter who curses her mother. Rivera's novel, on the other hand, shows the ways in which his people were held back by such superstitions: the threat that the earth would devour you for cursing God could easily be translated into a cautionary tale empowering Anglo packing shed owners or brutal foremen in the fields. The boy in *And the Earth Did Not Devour Him* learns this when he curses God and no punishment follows; in fact, the immediate effect of his blasphemy is that his father and younger brother, who are ill, begin to recover.

Rivera's type of literary realism and naturalism characterizes much Mexican American fiction and would seem to predominate over that other great style of American fiction, the romantic/gothic mode, situated in a borderland that Nathaniel Hawthorne once defined as "a neutral territory, somewhere between the real world and fairy-land, where the Actual and the Imaginary may meet." Perhaps not surprisingly, Joyce Carol Oates's recent anthology *American Gothic Tales* (1996) features no stories of the type collected in *Fantasmas,* that is "gothics" by Mexican American writers—nor any stories by Asian American or Native American writers either, and only one by an African American writer (Charles Johnson). Oates apologizes for the omission with the following statement: "I would have liked to include more stories by African-Americans and other American ethnic writers, but the 'gothic' has not been a popular mode among such writers, for the obvious reason that the 'real'—the America of social, political, and moral immediacy—is irresistibly compelling at this stage of their history."

Oates's qualification is right-hearted but wrong-headed, for she misses the clear fascination of Mexican American writers (in *Fantasmas* and elsewhere) with the supernatural in their works. In her influential study *Borderlands/La Frontera,* Gloria Anzaldúa charts her own personal rejection of the European dichotomy between the rational world and the supernatural world: "I allowed white rationality to tell me that the existence of the 'other world' was mere pagan superstition." Nevertheless, she begins to listen to these spirit voices and no longer denies their "reality." She calls this sensitivity to the other world "la facultad," and argues that those "who do not feel psychologically or psychically safe in the world are more apt to develop this sense— the tender, the homosexual of all races, the darkskinned, the outcast, the persecuted, the marginalized, the foreign."

Recent scholarship on minority literature confirms Anzaldúa's intuitions and goes further, showing how minority writers use supernatural themes in the creation of revisionist history. In *Cultural Hauntings: Ghosts and Ethnicity in Recent American Literature* (1998), Kathleen Brogan says, "Ghosts in contemporary ethnic literature function . . . to re-create ethnic identity through an imaginative recuperation of the past and to press this new version of the past into the service of the present." Supernatural stories by minority writers tell the story that the colonizer has both physically and psychically repressed. As Sandra Cisneros says of those voices silenced by the colonization of the Americas, "There is the necessary phase of dealing with these ghosts and voices most urgently haunting us, day by day."

That makes *Fantasmas* a necessary book, necessary for creating a place for these stories and for situating them in mainstream literary discussions. Many stories in *Fantasmas* come to mind as I quote Cisneros above, but most strongly the first story in the book, Carmen Tafolla's story "Tía." In that story a young woman finds herself (as did Gloria Anzaldúa) listening to those haunting voices, and quite naturally falls into communication with the spirit world: She hears "the in-and-out of breathing . . . more clearly each day, heard with something more than her ears, more than her heart, heard maybe with the life spirit that kept her going." The writers of *Fantasmas* write with that kind of sensibility, one which helps them make connections between the material and the spiritual world. This enables them to move beyond and between borders in all kinds of ways. The stories in *Fantasmas* vary greatly in approach and style, but they all make the same strong claim: that the supernatural must be seen as a part of reality, not as separate from it.

❧ ⊱═══⊰ ❧

In putting this book together over the last few years, I have had the support of many writers, editors, and educators. I thank first the writers who contributed to the book and patiently saw it through its evolution, in particular David Rice and Kathleen Alcalá, who supported the project at key stages. For support from The University of Texas-Pan American,

I would like to thank Dr. Rodolfo Rocha, Dr. Patricia De La Fuente, and Dr. George Avellano, who awarded me a UTPA scholar's grant that facilitated the editing of the book. Another faculty member, Elsa Saeta, provided me with an excellent reading list that, early on, helped me to focus the theme of the book. *Fantasmas* is dedicated to my creative writing students at The University of Texas–Pan American. Their knowledge of traditional tales and their twenty-first century sophistication about popular literary forms—and their willingness to breed the former with the latter—provided the catalyst for this collection.

INTRODUCTION

Kathleen Alcalá

When I saw the announcement for *Fantasmas*, my first thought was Why haven't *I* been asked to contribute to this? After all, *my* work has been reviewed in *The New York Review of Science Fiction.* How fantastic is that? But those were my secret thoughts. And secret thoughts are what these stories are all about.

Soon enough, Rob Johnson found me and soothed my ego by asking me to write this introduction, for which I am delighted.

Fantasmas are a particular kind of writing that is very popular in Mexico. My guess is that it is popular all over the world, as it serves as a bridge between traditional storytelling and pulp fiction, incorporating elements of both. Alberto Manguel has collected two volumes' worth of fantastic literature in *Black Water* and *Black Water 2*, published by Clarkson Potter. In some cases, the stories take the reader right over the line to horror, the worst thing you can imagine fulfilled. In others, the fantastic elements are merely implied, and if the reader tried to pinpoint the specific elements that made the story fantastic, it would be impossible to do. Rather, the fantastic element lies in "the overall effect" that Edgar Allan Poe tried to infuse into each of his stories.

In Latin America, there hasn't necessarily been a clear line between fantastic literature and literary fiction. This has allowed writers like Jorge Luis Borges, Gabriel García Márquez, and Clarice Lispector to be noticed by upstanding and respectable critics of modern culture, and has led to the eventual translation of their work, as well as that of many others. They now form a canon of work against which all the rest of us must be compared, although in many cases, we have little in common with them other than the Spanish language.

As far as I know, this is the first collection of fantastic literature specifically by Mexican Americans, and it contains elements that make these stories unlike any others. These stories are not, for example, mostly inspired by American and European written forms, as are the "standard" published Latin American *cuentos de fantasma*. If forced to generalize about specific elements that make the border stories chosen for this collection unique, I would include the following: (1) basis in oral tradition, (2) influence of folk religions, (3) use of vernacular forms, (4) influence of life and culture from the U.S. side of the border.

Unfortunately, some of these elements will be seen by critics as reinforcing certain much-avoided stereotypes in Mexican American literature. For example, an early manuscript reader of this book commented, "Serious Mexican American short story writers have been struggling their entire careers to create work that does not fit the stereotype that 'all Mexican American literature is about *curanderos, la llorona, tortillas*, and family superstitions.'" I think this response says more about the reviewer than the book itself, but it gives us a chance to talk about some very interesting things.

My parents' generation had to spend a great deal of time convincing people that Mexicans were capable of holding jobs outside the level of farm worker or menial laborer, and part of this was showing an "advanced" view of the world. In the forties and fifties, this meant being very patriotic, giving your children "American" (British) names and not appearing to be too superstitious or backwards. In other words, it was a class thing, and being Mexican was equated with being lower class. Of course it still is, but the ability of the writers in this collection to look at these symbols with irony, affection, and an eye toward their aesthetic value shows a generational shift in aesthetic viewpoint, from encouraging the production of literature depicting Mexican Americans in a socially acceptable light (the society being white), to our literature being written to express all that our culture has to offer, and not really caring what others think of us as a result.

My own relationship to this type of story spans generations of Mexicans and Mexican Americans.

In my library there is a book called *Relatos: misterio y realismo*, published in Mexico in 1947 and written by a distant relative of mine named José García Rodríguez. Each of his stories tells of ordinary people who go about their business and have an encounter, or near encounter, with the fantastic. In almost every case, the protagonist is saved from disaster by behaving in a decent or just manner. These are tales with morals: the weak are prey to the devil. But there is also an element of coincidence—had he taken this road rather than that—in the stories, as exemplified by "Michele's Miracle" by Kelly Jácquez in *Fantasmas*. What, really, is fate, and what control do we have over it?

While written in a manner that was probably modern for their time, the roots of García Rodríguez's stories in the folk tales of Mexico are evident. Universally, folk tales have been used to educate and entertain, to show acceptable behavior by example, and perpetuate the ways of a particular culture. In other words, these are didactic tales, and they have their roots, in turn, in mythology.

This is the way we explain the world to ourselves and each other. It is how we teach our young to survive.

García Rodríguez was a relative of mine, so the stories he was hearing and retelling are not too different from the folk history of my immediate family. As my sister pointed out to a group of "ladies who lunch" in Fargo, North Dakota, while they were discussing one of my more cryptic stories, what is *not* told is often as important as what *is* told in these stories. The imagination must be given free reign for these stories to work, and that is what gives them their universality and staying power. Unlike a television series that is forgotten the next season— except for *Star Trek*, of course, which a friend who is a professor of com-

parative literature insists is all taken from *The Odyssey*—*cuentos* of this
nature can be retold again and again without losing their punch.

Rob Johnson generated some of these stories by asking his students
to take folktales and retell them in a modern setting. While the stories
still retain their timelessness, this introduced two elements that I really
enjoy: the urban legend and modern dialect. Growing up in San
Bernardino, we had the urban legend of the White Albino. The name
for this person is redundant, one of the great things about this story. He
escaped from prison, where he was serving time for murder. He lived in
the San Bernardino Mountains, where he saved a young couple from
certain death in a snowstorm, murdered them, or almost murdered
them, and they drove away with the hook that he used instead of a hand
in the handle of the car . . .

Wait a minute, you say. This sounds familiar. Of course. It's an
urban legend, with all of the elements of fear and mystery *of that particular place* introduced—incarceration, the mountains, being caught
out late with your boyfriend, and extra-white people. The ambiguous
nature of the White Albino is what makes the story linger in the mind.
Did he mean them harm, or was he trying to help them? Can we judge
people by their looks? Their color? Their past?

The power of place—a crucial element of the literature of the West
and Southwest—is evident in all of the stories in *Fantasmas*. By using
local, modern dialect, these stories are tied to landscape and culture in
a way that draws on the rich imagery of our everyday lives. Like the
house with the blinds always drawn, or the cross and flowers by the
roadside, each feature of our landscape embodies a story. By their language, you can see these girls with their big hair and painted nails, these
guys in their skinny jeans, and know that, yes, things like this happen
to regular people—people like you, or at least what you used to be like
when you were young and skinny. Reading these stories will make you
recall half a dozen more, and that's the point of literature—to tell and
retell the stories that make us human, to dip into the common well of
our consciousness and bring up a detail that links us to each other.

One aspect of fantastic literature that must be noted is its political
content. Starting with Alejo Carpentier in Cuba, who probably first

used the term "magic realism," such fiction has been used as a vehicle for conveying political and social truths that could be fatal if presented more baldly. In spite of their careful eloquence, many of its practitioners have lived out their lives in exile as a result of their work. This is the extraordinary power of the written word: that it can make dictators, surrounded by militia, tremble in their boots. In *Fantasmas*, the dictators have been transformed into packing shed bosses, abusive husbands, and the turbulent desires of the heart.

Apparently, when we talk about magic, we talk about love. As Torie Olson writes in "Tear Out My Heart," "There is a milagro for every body part, but only the hearts come in super size. It appears that, more than anything else, people are sick at heart." These stories are in large part about desire—what we really want and what we will do to get it. In many cases, extreme sexuality, violence, and revenge are linked to supernatural powers, some incarnation of the devil, as in "Lilith's Dance" by Gary G. Hernández. These stories talk about our hidden impulses, and throughout history, I'm sure, these tales have been used as an outlet for the parts of the subconscious over which we feel we have no control. The implication is that these devils are contained within each of us, and we must strive every day to contain them. In our particular blend of pragmatism and mysticism, the person in the story might ask the Devil if he takes Visa before beginning to bargain.

There are no gauzy angels in these modern interpretations, no apparitions of the Virgin Mary, or bleeding icons. Rather, we must be angels to one another, we must incarnate the good as well as the bad. As Stephanie Reyes points out in "Bad Debts and Vindictive Women," these tales, traditionally, are supposed to have a moral. After reading them, I thought about this and decided that, if there is a common moral to the stories in *Fantasmas*, it is this: If you love someone, don't forget to tell them. Because when it's your time, it's your time.

So light some candles, put on some *té de canela* (you don't have to drink it—smelling it is good enough) and let us tell you about women with burning lips, men with long knives, and why you should never put a frog between your legs. . . .

TÍA

Carmen Tafolla

WHEN SHE WAS 82, SHE LOST HER EYESIGHT. CATARACTS. SAME YEAR, she lost her husband. Two years later, the cholesterol and blood sugar were responsible for a severe loss of hearing. The niece that took care of her was the one whom everyone turned to when someone got sick. Nice lady. Let her move in and cooked for her, con mucho cariño. Husband said, "Oh, well. It's just like when we had our babies. I don't mind."

By 89, she was having some serious problems with the diabetes. In two years, she lost two legs. "It's OK," said the niece, "I'll take care of her. She doesn't need to walk." But then the different parts of her started falling off. By 96, the whole day was bathing, giving medicine, changing diapers, and listening to groans. The night was worse. The husband left. The niece was now taking care of her aunt, an older sister, and her father. The aunt began to cough and some internist said she should be in the hospital. So they put her in. The niece came by every evening. Covered her with a bathrobe that only had to cover a shape two and a half feet long. The doctor said it wouldn't be long.

But after two months, the doctor had been transferred to a different hospital, and one of his eager and eminent replacements had dropped dead of a heart attack.

In the third month, the hospital social worker recommended that she be moved to the "extended care" unit. The niece still came every evening, sitting by her side, holding the space that used to be her hand, and finally checking her watch and going home with a sigh to prepare for her father's doctor visits the next day. "I feel like running away from home," she said, "but there's no one to take care of everyone. Nobody who'll do it. They'd all come hunt me down to do the family chores. Sometimes this sitting by Tía's side is the only quiet time I have."

The hospital social worker was reassigned to a different unit; faces came and faces went. When they had to weigh her, they used the baby scales. She was under 40 pounds. "She can't last much longer," said the young doctor, new to the beat and soon to be gone.

She didn't speak anymore, but she coughed and she groaned, and the night nurse said to the niece, "Prepare yourself, honey; she doesn't have long. But she's going to a better place." After a while, the night nurse went on to a better position with a private foundation. Finally, Medicare said they couldn't cover any more hospital days that year. So her niece came with a lap blanket, wrapped her gently, and carried her home.

The niece was having chest pains regularly these days and her own children had all moved out of state. Her grandchildren were asking what she was going to leave them, what the market value of her house was, and if she had a DNR order. A living will?

The niece changed the diapers more easily now that the aunt's weight had dropped even more. And the other sick family members had passed on and released her of her extra duties. The ex-husband never came by. And the brothers and sisters that had been too busy to take care of the aunt were still too busy to take care of the niece.

The niece lit a vela once a week right after her trip to the grocery store, but soon she had made arrangements with a teenage neighbor to run the errands for her for a small fee. Life got quieter, and the niece quit counting the years going by. Sometimes she felt that the only thing

that got her up each morning was the knowledge that she had to change
the diaper and prepare the corn atole. Atole that she spoon-fed her tía,
and occasionally tasted a spoonful of as well.

But finally the morning came when the clock had wound down,
the spirit had run out, and the niece did not rise from her bed.

The house was quiet for a long time.

❧ ⊱——⊰ ☙

"Well, it's old but I'm really happy with it. A good place for graduate
work. You wouldn't believe this place! It's really, well . . . I dunno . . .
like home. Una casita chiquita, calladita, but it's got something . . .

"And there's a vela to the Virgin of Guadalupe at a little altar and
hand-crocheted doilies on the couch. Yeah, I got it with the furniture
and everything. There's gobs of stuff here! The family didn't think a
garage sale would be worth the trip down here, so they sold the whole
thing at a flat rate and great terms, even let me move in right away
and prorate the rent . . . I can hardly wait to open up some of these
trunks!"

She was right. The place was cozy. She noticed it changed her
lifestyle right from the beginning. She started buying candles to the
Virgin of Guadalupe and lighting them at the altar, and for some reason, she began cooking atole. There were so many pillows piled on the
bed in the second bedroom, and several of them seemed to be antiques.
She promised herself to get to that room as soon as she cleared away
some of the stuff in the kitchen.

By the end of the first week, she was feeling the rhythm of the
house, and at night she was dreaming—of a flow like the ocean's tide—
an in and out, a soothing repetitive pattern that sounded like life itself,
like breathing. She quit working on the dissertation and began writing
in her journal—writing between pots of atole or sartenes of frijol con
queso, and sometimes a homemade caldo steeped all day till the nutri-
ents filled the air, and she felt she could almost inhale their sustenance.
And the dreams of tides, of ins and outs, of the breath of life, began to
fill her waking hours as well.

One night, in the middle of the night she dreamed she was walk-ing to the second bedroom and opening the trunk, peering inside, and seeing things she recognized from long, long ago. She even picked it up, this thing she had never touched, but had somehow never forgotten. It was rounded and pulsing and smelled of corn being toasted, warmed, prepared. Then she had approached the bed and looked beyond the pil-lows until her own breathing had tied her to the universe. In the morning, she couldn't remember if she had really gone to that room or merely dreamed of it.

The months passed. Her sense of peace deepened. There were three constants in life: the atole, the vela to the Virgin of Guadalupe, and the in-and-out of breathing that she heard more and more clearly each day, heard with something more than her ears, more than her heart, heard maybe with the life spirit that kept her going. She or the house or the air—or maybe someone else—was breathing.

By the time she met the niece's aunt, there was no surprise inside her. There was only the desire to cook atole and the dedication to con-tinue the breath of the ocean's life. If she could keep her alive, she could keep the universe alive. Tía was tiny by now, no more than an armful. And there was nothing left to lose except her heartbeat and that obsti-nate, soothing breath.

She fed her atole, or maybe the old woman inhaled it. All she knew was that the rhythms of her life had changed, and they followed the inhale and the exhale of the large cloudy brown eyes. When she was not cooking or buying velas, she wrote. And when she had ceased to light velas, the person who followed her read the writings.

These writings.

⚜ ╞══╡ ⚜

And they knew that if you listened very closely, you could hear her inhale, the universe, still alive. Do you hear it? Do you hear it now? Between the flickers of the vela in your living room. Between your foot-steps as you walk to the kitchen, thinking of smooth life-giving atole—thinking of sustenance so soft, so strong you can inhale it, in the parti-cles of the air, thinking of . . . life. . . .

OUR STORY FRAYS

Rubén Degollado

EMILIANO CONTRERAS WRITHED LIKE A SNAKE BEFORE HE DIED. Over pan dulce and coffee, over iced tea at China Palace, over a bonfire and beer, we Izquierdos hear many versions and this is the only immutable truth. It is the only thing that comforts us.

A week before Contreras died, God or the Devil had revealed this to him in a dream. After his revelation, he confessed to Father Guerra at St. Joseph the Worker the indiscretions and the brujería he had worked on people, especially our family, all of these decades. His daughter Lina came over that Saturday afternoon and told Abuela Guadalupe that he had completed most of the prescribed penance, and he felt all he had to do was to be forgiven by her. Lina gave our grandmother instructions she did not know how to read and left.

Accounts being what they are, like statements after an accident, people must choose sides. Either we believe what Abuela and Tía Victoria told us, or we believe what we know. Why did she honor Contreras's request after all he had done? This man had been responsible for our abuelo Papa Tavo's mental illness and ultimately his death.

5

Some of us agree with Abuela, that being the good woman that she is, she wanted only to forgive him. In this version, she called Victoria for a ride so that she could help pray with her. If this were completely true, why didn't she call her own sons or daughters? we ask. She could have called Big Cirilo, her own son, our tío, who calls himself a prayer warrior. We ask ourselves why, being such a devout Catholic, she chose sin vergüenza Tía Victoria, who flirts with our cousin Cirilo, who never finishes the Apostle's Creed because it becomes too Catholic after the Trinity part. The truth we do not admit, but are certain of, is that she called Victoria, not for her gift of tongues or because she liked her, but because she knew she needed her help in ending Contreras. Tía Victoria was supposed to be there. She, more than Abuela, was the one who killed Contreras.

Victoria pulled up to Abuela Guadalupe's house in her new forest green Mustang. Although we do not like to think of her that way, we picture Victoria as she stood under the garage waiting for Abuela to lock the burglar bars, her thick Indian hair over her shoulders, looking good even in her baggy blue nursing scrubs.

They said their saludos and Victoria helped Abuela into the front seat, which was so low to the ground our grandmother felt as if she were sinking. We see Abuela in the black lace widow's rebozo she now wears in church. Victoria wore her nursing uniform and silver rings that glimmer like stars on all her fingers. We see them as they drove away in that beautiful car with the illegal tints.

Some of us are satisfied that the sons of Contreras died early, violent deaths, as if we had been gifted with vengeance before the hechizos took their toll on us. The oldest son, Emilio, must have looked, instead of ducked, because a 7.62 X 39 round went through his helmet and took off the top of his head, dappling the jungle leaves of Vietnam with bits of brains and Contreras blood. The younger one, Gregorio, was found floating in an irrigation canal in Mission a few years ago. The cause of death was undetermined to the authorities, but not unknown to us. Contreras's sons did not live for the same reason Papa Tavo died madly gibbering at San Juan's Nursing Home, not knowing who he was, knowing only that he wanted a cigarette we could never give him.

Same reason Uncle Demetrio has been in and out of suicide watch at Charter Palms for the last ten years. Same reason our cousin Joey is only twenty-six and already he's tried Paxil, Prozac, and Tofranil and nothing seems to pull him out of the depression. Same reason Oso Negro hasn't worked for Joey's father. Same reason Tía Dina hasn't been able to leave the house since Abuelo died and all she does is read the Psalms, pray the rosary all day, and worry Eusebio and the girls.

All of this sadness in both bloodlines, Contreras and Izquierdo, has happened because that demonio Contreras cursed his family by cursing ours. Besides the hechizos he was paid to do, he threw bottles of urine into our yard, which we hear is an old curse that is supposed to ruin your enemy's crops and dirty their seed forever. He burned black candles to Satanás, praying that the little fortune from our abuelo's painting and drywall business would abandon us. He severed the cloven hoof of a goat and buried it, among other things, under Abuela's bedroom window. Because of this entierro, El Diablo walked around in her dreams, never giving her peace until one of us finally dug it up. The last maldición we know about was the entierro that Gonzalo and a curandero unearthed and burned last winter. It was a photo of Gonzalo and Abuelo leaning against the new red Ford they had just bought. They lost this truck after Abuelo had the first nervous breakdown.

We barely recognize Papa Tavo from copies of this picture. He beams, his Stetson tilted at a cocky angle, his strong dark hands resting on the shiny hood. For those of us who knew him too late, we can only remember his mouth the way it looked from the hospital bed, our women wiping the spittle away from his lips. We remember only the fear of our mothers asking us to go to Papa Tavo to give him our saludos. As we stand in that room of our minds, we see his long wooden fingernails anticipating their growth beyond his death. All that keeps us from dwelling on this is Gonzalo's hard, immortal stare.

In his white T-shirt and khakis, he seems to say, Chinga tu madre, güey. Pinche Contreras, I will outlive you. And my wife, a woman, will destroy you. How you like that?

It is unknown how Contreras got the photograph, but he stabbed nails through their chests and wrapped the frame in plastic. We do not understand his black ways, but we think Contreras meant to crucify us and bind our souls from being resurrected. If Gonzalo and the curandero had not stopped his magic, we cannot imagine what he would have done to Abuelo's grave.

When they got to Lina's house, we imagine both of them prayed for different things. Tía Victoria, in that babble she calls prayer languages, said words that no one but Little Gonzalo could have interpreted.

One day, the poor kid said to us, "Did you know that 'turroco' means holy?"

We said, "Did you know that the word 'gullible' isn't in the dictionary?"

And Little Gonzalo, who loves to draw and read, said, "Really?" and went looking for a dictionary as we laughed about it. We felt bad about this when he looked up the definition and we saw that expression we remember on our own faces. All of us were relieved when Little Gonzalo agreed to throw the football around with us afterward. We did not like seeing our cousin hurt, and none of us wanted to answer to Gonzalo if the kid went crying to him.

Here is where our story frays, and we must choose a thread to unravel it all.

We hear Abuela Guadalupe in her lispy storytelling Spanish. All the way up to the door, she said to give her strength to forgive this man, to let it all sink into the sea of forgetfulness, to wash away any drop of unforgiveness in her heart. We wonder if she meant it.

We see Lina's house as they walked inside. It was impressive with the bounce and smell of freshly laid carpet and new white paint. Both of them thought that this was not the house of a brujo's daughter, of a neighborhood slut that once put out like some cantina prostitute. Where were the black candles, cobwebs, rooster feet, bottles of piss, malas hierbas? No, the house was well lit and clean, maybe a little tacky because of too many brass knickknacks, maybe smelling like this morning's barbacoa. Gilded picture frames of fat, hopeful nieces smiling for their own confirmations, quinceañeras, and weddings decorated the walls.

Lina explained that she had been looking for Señora Izquierdo all day, calling around for her or Gonzalo's number and driving around the block by her old house.

Abuela explained that her daughter, our tía Marisol, had asked her to come along with her to the boticas in Reynosa to buy diet pills, and that they had stopped at a taquería before they crossed back. She apologized although she did not need to, although she should not have.

Lina told them that her father had been waiting for them in the back bedroom. We picture Contreras in the darkness as he searched the thick shadows for the death angel.

Lina called her father and said that Señora Izquierdo and her daughter had arrived. Her daughter, they both thought, and realized that Lina did not even know who her father had been cursing.

Lina turned on the lamp and Abuela saw Contreras up close for the first time in years. His spotted brown head shone blue from the alley light. Greasy smears and the lamp glare on his glasses hid his eyes. Abuela probably thought, This was the man that killed my husband? He sat up nervously and all he wore were chinos and an undershirt worn thin. His gut hung over his pants and they could see his saggy old man's breasts through the gray cotton.

Contreras told them, "Pásale, pásale. I am so happy you came."

He did not waste time and told them he was sorry for being jealous of them for all these years. It wasn't Octavio's fault that the Contrerases had to go pick fruit with the seasons while the Izquierdo family got to live in the same place all year round. He apologized about selling them to the Devil, and wept in the pathetic way of men we had tried to ignore in the nursing homes.

"I would take it back if I could," he blubbered. "All I can do is end it and pay the blood payment with my own life." He went on to explain that it was revealed to him that the curses on the Izquierdos would somehow die with the sons of Octavio, but there would still have to be a reckoning.

We agree.

He asked Abuela if she could forgive him. We see her face. She had creases and dark circles under her tired eyes from so much lost sleep and happiness. But they are, and were, peaceful as we first remember them at Abuelo's funeral.

She never grieved like other widows we had seen. She did not lean into the casket and grip Papa Tavo, her lamentations forcing the family to turn away, to step outside for a cigarette. She sat in the front pew of Ceballos's funeral home, consoling *us*, saying that it was better that he was finally resting. Abuela Guadalupe's tiny knuckles folding and unfolding a handkerchief spoke that there would be no more terrified late-night calls to Gonzalo during full moons. On such nights, Abuelo would no longer tear the house apart looking for black objects to destroy. Somehow, Contreras had made Papa Tavo believe that anything black emanated evil. Times like this, even Gonzalo, who is stronger and meaner than all of his brothers, could not subdue him. This was also the reason we could never keep him in one nursing home for more than a month. One time we know of, Gonzalo just let him go, because Abuelo looked especially crazed, even possessed. To scare Gonzalo, it must have been something more than usual. Our grandfather ransacked drawers and lifted the mattresses, and they could not understand why the toaster from Christmas, Lalo's stereo, the remote controls or Abuela's chanclas did not satisfy him. He went to the TV room and turned over a corduroy recliner they had bought at a yard sale. Papa Tavo ripped the white gauze from the bottom and howled when he looked inside. The story goes—and we believe Abuela and Tío Gonzalo—that the steel frame inside formed a black crucifix. He knew this without ever having looked at it.

That night in the dry fields past Barrio La Balboa, about five miles from Mexico, they burned the chair and threw what was left into a canal, speaking unmentioned prayers and curses. In the pauses between words, Abuela heard a mass of whispers she could not understand coming from the flames, and later from beneath the black water.

I forgive you for everything you have done. She said this despite looking into Contreras's face and remembering Papa Tavo's, how he looked so catatonic in the front seat, watching her burn the curse without relief or understanding.

"Thank you, thank you," he said through his stuffed nose. "God bless you, God bless you," as if he needed to tell her she was blessed. At some point, he asked her if she would please pray the rosary with him. We know it was because he did not know the Apostle's Creed or the Order of the Mysteries or the Glory Be to the Father because he had not gone to mass since he sold his soul. Contreras was trying to use her again as if she were one of his 17th Street prostitutes.

After raising so many, Abuela knows the needs of men, but not their motives. Or she just did not care. Because she chose not to use one of Lina's candles, Abuela had brought one in her purse. She set it on the nightstand and lit it. Lina and Victoria stood mute, not certain what to do, but pleased by the candle's warmth. Out of respect, because Abuela asked with her eyes, Victoria agreed to kneel like the Catholic she used to be, but only prayed unintelligible words. We are not sure what Lina did.

Abuela prayed the Our Fathers and Hail Marys in her whisper that calms us. Our grandmother was dignified and painless on the Italian tiles. She managed not to shift knees or wince because of her visions of celestial ecstasy. Abuela saw herself with Saint Teresa and Saint Catherine, floating in the air with the Holy Spirit, her old body not weighing her down, not collecting fluid and burning in her knees. Contreras wept as she prayed. "Perdóneme, forgive me, Señora Izquierdo."

When they were finished, he did not presume to hug our grandmother, but instead reached for her hand. We do not like to think of those hands that had handled unholy entrails and whores touching our grandmother. His eyes red and greasy, he said, "Gracias," and shook her hand.

Abuela said, "I could do nothing else."

He said that he felt better and he was ready for God or the Devil to take him.

He hugged his daughter, who was probably kneeling now, and she said, "It's over, Papi, it's over." She too had lost everyone, and she hoped that her father's visions were not true even though she knew she was lying to herself. Then the brujo looked at Victoria. We do not know if Victoria asked for it, or if she was appalled at the idea. But Contreras could not resist. She was so lovely and young, with girlish features—a small pushed-up nose, black eyes close together and that Mexica hair like a shadow that must have taken him back to his youth in Mexico. We see him as he opened his arms to embrace her. Victoria leaned into him and gave a piece of herself to save us all.

He held her too tightly and it scared her, his old-man stink and evil at lover's length. To protect herself, Victoria reached behind him and stroked his head, her fingers lingering over his ear. We see his sick, bloated face as he enjoyed this. Lina could not believe this, although Abuela always knew what was about to happen, and had even planned on it.

Victoria put her mouth close to his ear and whispered something that neither of them could understand. At first he smiled, all quivery, and she laughed a little, but then his spirit knew. His body went limp, and the women rushed forward to help.

Victoria said, "Give him room to breathe," and she checked his pulse, his breathing, and his ghost inside. Lina probably agreed because Victoria was a nurse with those clothes and her name tag. She held Contreras in her arms, his yellow eyes opened to her black. Under his clothes, Tía felt his flesh quiver, and she accepted what she had done. She did not let go and tried to hide from Lina what was roiling in her eyes.

Contreras lay there in silence and surrender until a low hum in his chest grew into a groan. He coughed and they heard phlegm rattle and he convulsed with the effort. Then he vomited a little, his white tongue stretching out of his heavy face.

As Victoria searched for something to wipe his mouth, his midsection jerked upward like a striking snake, only his head and feet remaining on the floor. Abuela gasped and crossed herself as she heard something crack inside. His body unbowed and slapped to the tiles, and his skin rippled long after it should have stopped. Victoria held him the whole time, calmly ignoring the worming of his flesh under her touch.

The wave began in his toes. Between the bands of his sandals, they saw them curl. It moved up into his legs, and his body began to writhe back and forth, except he did not go anywhere, and the motion was too fluid for a human.

He looked at them bug-eyed from another realm, and said, "Por favor. Ayúdenme." They looked on and did nothing but watch his body squirm and shiver.

Lina rushed to him again, but all she did was tug at his pant leg, wailing, "¡APÁ, APÁ!" With eyes veiled by the rebozo, Abuela crossed herself, rubbed her rosary beads, and prayed for it not to be too painful. If she had chosen to, we know she could have prayed for it to stop, and it would have.

"¡PERDÓNENME. PERDÓNENME!" he cried out as some new pang grew within. "¡DÉJENME!"

We imagine Victoria stroked his hair and caressed his cheek, holding him like her own. She said, "Sshh, sshh, sshh. It will pass and then it will be OK."

When she did this, Contreras tried to say something else. He hissed through his teeth, spitting into Victoria's face. She wiped it off and rubbed it into her pant leg with her finger tips.

"SsssssSS. . . . SsssssSS. . . . Sssssssssss." The last hiss died down like the last of gas escaping, as if some part of Contreras had given up. There was horror and confusion on his face because he could not speak. He needed to complete his word, perhaps one final curse, and he knew they had finally come for him. He closed his eyes, gulped, and settled. They listened as his breathing subsided and leaked into silence. Victoria leaned down to him, her hair brushing and covering his wet face. She turned her ear to his open mouth as if she expected Contreras to make some final confession.

Both Abuela Guadalupe and Tía Victoria told us this story over beer with Gonzalo softly singing corridos and strumming an out-of-tune guitar. We do not know exactly when we heard it, but remember it best with the fire flickering on their faces.

Abuela explains that Contreras had completed Father Guerra's penance, and that the writhing before his death was a struggle for his soul. God won and San Pedro let him into the kingdom of God, she assures us.

Tía Victoria explains that although she could not interpret the prayer language, she thinks the Spirit within her rebuked the demons and told Contreras the truth about having to ask God, and not Abuela, for forgiveness. According to her, his response like a hiss was his trying to say the beginning of the word 'saved' or the ending of 'Jesús,' words that meant he had asked for forgiveness from the only true source. Neither of them is sure, but our grandmother and Tía Victoria agree

they felt a spirit of peace descend in the room after he took his last
breath.

To their faces, we agree with their story of his redemption. We say,
"Pues sí, pues sí," but we do not believe them. They lie, not to deceive
us, but so that the burden of what they had to do will not be placed on
our backs as well. Abuela Guadalupe and Tía Victoria look at each
other when they assure us of his salvation, and a secret passes between
their black eyes glinting in the firelight. It is something they will never
say and we will never ask about. Through the smoke, though, we see
what they are protecting us from, that they do not want to change our
lives forever. We see what they cannot hide. Shadows of the women
they had to be dance inside their burning vision. These dark others
seduced Contreras to writhe like the serpent he was, trampled him
under their bare, blackened heels, and threw him into the fires of
Gehena, wailing and weeping the whole time.

CANTINFLAS

Stephen D. Gutiérrez

CANTINFLAS HUNG FROM THE STRINGS OF A WOODEN CROSS.

His feet dangled in midair. His shiny black costume, painted on with meticulous care, displayed white etchings and silver braids that made him look like a skeleton at times. His grand sombrero was ludicrous, with flowery curlicues outlining the brim.

He smiled with an upturned cherry-red mouth.

A perky, adept mustache adorned his lip.

Red spots dotted his cheeks.

Cantinflas hung in the corner of Steve's room. Steve was the little Mexican American boy who kept him. He kept him safe from all the other little toys and animals on his shelves and window frames.

He bought him on Olvera Street for a dollar.

Cantinflas hung from a bedpost.

Steve played with him.

One day he took him down from his spot in midair and started dancing with him on the rug.

"Ándale, ándale," he said, making him move to the rhythms of a song he made up in his head. He put a penny down and started enacting the Mexican hat dance, using Cantinflas as a dancer and the penny as a sombrero.

"Ándale, ándale," he said, with a thick American accent. "¡Muévete!"

Then Cantinflas stopped. "¿Por qué?" he asked and looked over his shoulder at the other animals.

They were getting restless on the shelves.

One leaped down and the rest followed him.

Slowly they transformed into their true selves. They shed their furry fluffiness to become snarling, terrifying beasts.

They pushed Steve back into the corner of his room where he lay cowering under a bright poster of the circus.

Madonna was riding an elephant with a hand waving to the crowd.

A rock star in a poster near her was spitting into a mike.

An athlete jumping up to a basketball hoop said this was the breakfast of champions.

Steve's room was a pleasantly painted place of peace and serenity threatened by the crazy beasts in front of him.

He cowered under his arms, hiding the sight before him.

Cantinflas was the biggest threat to Steve. Every time Steve peeked out, Cantinflas got bigger and bigger.

Cantinflas grew.

Then he changed. He transformed into an alligator man.

He stood in his greenness in front of Steve, in his stovepipe hat tattered and torn with ludicrous slippers flapping on the ends of his feet.

He stunk.

He talked Alligator talk.

By this he meant bayou talk.

"Bayou I talk, bayou I live, you son of a bitch." And he ate Steve.

A pool of blood formed under his alligator toes.

They were hard and clawlike.

The pool of blood was gross and disgusting.

All the other animals jumped in willingly to rend what they could of Steve.

He floundered in the muck getting thicker, getting thinner by degrees of frenzy.

The animals tore at him.

His arm flailed, and then was lost.

This was terrible!

Steve yelped, "Alligator Land! Alligator Land!" as he succumbed to the last terrible gnashing of the animals destroying him, devouring him, ending him. He died and went to heaven, Alligator Heaven, where he stood in front of a portrait of an Alligator Man in a cobra-hooded throne sneering at him.

He had to throw darts at Uncle Sam.

Oh, it was awful; too, too awful for Steve to contemplate too much longer, and he came out of his dream in a touchdown he scored for his local high school.

That was years later.

The referee blew a whistle.

When he woke up his father was shaking his shoulder, Cantinflas was on his side with an arm missing, and the sun was coming up above the clouds that smelled of cocoa puffs and burnt toast.

THE GIFT

Jacquie Moody

WHEN LUPITA TURNED FIFTEEN, HER GRANDMOTHER DECIDED IT was time to give her the gift. The girl was almost a woman in age, but her body was still that of a child: she was round where she should be flat, and flat where she should be round. The grandmother had received the gift at fifteen as well, and it certainly worked for her. The girl definitely needed to marry soon and leave home to start a family of her own. The prospect of marriage was grim as long as little Lupita was trapped in that child body of hers.

The grandmother sighed. Qué triste, she thought, that often our outsides don't do our insides justice.

<hr/>

The quinceañera was a joyous occasion. Lupita looked like a plump little bride in her white lace gown. Her grandmother had sewn the gown herself on her new Singer. The backyard was strung with white Christmas lights that twinkled like little stars—just for Lupita, tonight, a swirling sun in the center of a tiny universe. She danced with Tío

Humberto, with the boys from Catholic school. She even danced with
her big sister's boyfriend, Antonio, who winked at her playfully when
the dance ended, and then proceeded to chase her across the lawn with
threats of imminent "tickle-torture."

The picnic table beneath the big oak tree was draped with a paper
tablecloth and covered with brightly wrapped gifts. Her grandmother
gave her two gifts, both wrapped in shiny red cellophane left over from
last Easter. Lupita tore the paper from the first gift, a tiny box. From
inside she pulled a glittering crystal rosary that caught the light and
scattered into a hundred fireflies. Lupita placed the necklace over her
head. The crucifix dangled between the small mounds of her pre-
pubescent breasts. When she reached for the second gift, her
grandmother clasped her hand.

"Save that one for later." She winked and took Lupita's face into her
hands, kissing each of her cheeks.

"You're a woman now, mi reina."

Lupita yawned and surveyed the lawn strewn with empty Lone Star
bottles and white streamers. Holding the hem of her lace dress, she
crept through the den, where the men had gathered and were downing
shots of Herradura and past the kitchen where the women were huddled like birds around a table of empanadas and fresh coffee.

Her older sister, Isabella, was sitting at the top of the stairs with
Antonio.

"Just where do you think *you're* going, Lupita?"

"To bed." Lupita faked an exaggerated yawn.

She shut her bedroom door behind her. The second gift was now
sitting on her vanity. She picked it up and shook it. It was definitely a
bottle. She peeled off the red paper. The contents of the bottle were
pink, like Pepto Bismol or the liquid soap in the restrooms at school.
She wrinkled her nose at the thought. A crude manila label wound
around the bottle embossed with blotched type: AMOR. She opened
the bottle and a scent engulfed her, reminding her instantly of
Valentines and scented silk roses, or the candles in San Fernando

Cathedral. The backside of the label instructed her to PORE INTIRE
CONTENTS INTO HOT BATH AND SOKE FOR ONE HOUR.

Lupita turned on the bathtub faucet and sat in her bathrobe at the
edge of the porcelain tub. As she watched the tub fill with steaming
water, a sadness came over her. She was fifteen now, a woman, but she
still felt like a little girl. Something in the back of her mind kept asking
*What's the big deal? So Grandma went and bought me some pretty bath
stuff, why the big secret?* But this didn't look like anything you'd buy at
the mall. It came from the botanica, that was obvious. She'd heard
funny stories about stuff you bought from the botanica. She had been
there with her grandmother and seen the candles and crosses and the
lady with one eye who said *¡No toques nada!* if she even went near anything. That old lady gave her the creeps.

⚜ ⊱────⊰ ⚜

The liquid made curious little pink clouds in the bathwater, like upside-
down whirls of cotton candy. Lupita climbed into the bath. Her
pink-painted toenails peeked out of the water. She closed her eyes. She
was surprised, when she opened her eyes after a few minutes, to see that
the bathwater was clear again.

She waited an hour, as instructed. The bath water seemed to have
grown warmer. She stepped from the bath and looked into the steamy
mirror. The blurred form reflecting back did not look like her own. The
patches of steam on the mirror faded one at a time. As each patch disappeared, it revealed something new: an arm, a breast, a sliver of brown
torso. Slowly the parts formed a whole: a woman, slender, strong like a
jaguar, with a full bosom and long legs. She ran her hands in disbelief
over the newly formed curve of hips, the powerful thighs. Her skin
looked like her grandfather's café con leche. But it was Lupita, she was
somehow the same.

⚜ ⊱────⊰ ⚜

At first, no one really seemed to notice much of anything different
about Lupita. There were little things, however. Her mother began call-

ing her Lupe, as in: "*Lupe*, it's time we go shopping for something a little more *substantial*—those training bras aren't working anymore." Her
father looked up from his newspaper, and Lupita blushed.

Soon the boys at school began to treat her differently. Pencils and
spitballs were no longer aimed at the back of her long hair; instead,
anonymous love notes scrawled on loose-leaf paper were slipped
between the vents of her locker and into her books. At first their leering made her uncomfortable, but there were certainly advantages to it.
She no longer had to carry her books home, someone was always ready
to carry them for her. After a while, she didn't even have to walk home.
The junior and senior boys began offering her rides.

One day Antonio offered Lupe a ride home. Isabella was in Mexico
City for a whole week with an exchange program. Antonio was a senior,
wickedly handsome, with thick black hair like el diablo on the Lotería
cards. She had always harbored a secret crush on him. He winked at her
in the car, the wind whipping up his black hair, but the wink seemed
different than the big-brother teasing he'd subjected her to before. He
pulled his car into her front yard. No one was home.

"How do you spell your name, Lupita, your full name?"

"G-U-A-D-A-L-U-P-E."

Once inside, Antonio spelled "guadalupe" on her belly, using the
tip of his tongue for a pluma.

❧ ⊱———⊰ ❧

Lupita's face was ruddy from Antonio's rough kisses and unshaven cheeks.
She was staring dreamily at the chalkboard when Sister Mary Joseph
Hinojosa's ruler came down on her desk with a loud clap like lovers' bellies.

"Guadalupe Guevarra, you are blushing como una novia this morning. Are you ill, my child? Or do you perhaps have something to confess?"

Lupita said nothing.

"Well, then, maybe you should go to the chapel and think about it
for awhile."

Lupita shrugged and grudgingly left the classroom. Once in the
chapel, she knelt before the altar, her little heart full of shame, and recit-

ed ten Hail Marys. She was in the middle of number seven when she smelled smoke. Was this her punishment from God? Was the chapel on fire? She swung around and saw a shadowy figure huddled near the incense, puffing on a cigarette.

"I have to have at least one vice," said the figure as it emerged. Lupita gasped—it was Brother Devon Kinkaid, the young brother with the eyes like crisp new hundred dollar bills. He sat next to her on the pew. Lupita smiled, and her girlish giggling soon filled the chapel like the baroque curlicues of smoke coming from Brother Devon's cigarette.

She plucked the cigarette from between his lips, "Gimmie that, you ought to quit." She dragged deeply on the cigarette and exhaled like a caricature of someone twice her age. She quickly forgot about Antonio.

When Sister Hinojosa's sophomore religion class ended, she noticed that Lupita still hadn't returned to her desk.

❧ ╪═╪ ☙

This was how it began, and how it continued. The lovers grew in number, but Lupita loved them all equally. She knew how to please each one individually, and each she loved for a different reason. One made love and dinner with equal passion, filling her with exquisite food and wine like she'd never tasted before. Another showed her the world, sneaking her off to other cities on weekends while her friends covered for her, and even to Italy over Easter break. One she admired for his boyish grin, another for the panther-like sway of his androgynous hips. They ranged in age: from the chubby freshman with the big heart for whom she felt sorry, to the captain of varsity football, to her father's boss in his starched white shirts and squeaky Italian shoes.

❧ ╪═╪ ☙

If one could be sick with desire, she was, and it coursed through her veins like a cancer. She no longer went out with her friends. She couldn't concentrate in class, and soon started skipping school altogether. She refused to eat because food no longer satisfied her hunger.

Sometimes she would weep for hours because desire hurt. It was a quiet pain that began between her thighs and traveled up some vein to her heart, where it exploded. At night she would stand on her balcony and silently call out her lovers' names. Sometimes they answered her call, as if telepathically, and scaled the magnolia tree to make love to her amongst the teddy bears and pink ruffles of her bedroom. Other times, only the night would respond, and the ache would travel its slow course up to her chest, as every vein in her body cried out.

She thought of the convent, she thought of Sister Hinojosa, she wore her santos pinned to her 36C bra. The leering never ceased—she felt their eyes on her everywhere she went. She locked herself in her room. In the shower, she scrubbed her skin until it was pink, as if scrubbing would erode her fine features, but instead it gave her skin a rosy glow that only made her more attractive.

The grandmother was beginning to worry. Her granddaughter was in a constant state of fever now. She gave Lupita special teas, but the tea evaporated the minute it touched the girl's lips. She placed ice cubes on Lupita's head to cool her fever, but the ice cubes would melt instantly and slide down her cheeks like tears. The grandmother was at her wit's end. Her gift had gone awry. A milky, clouded egg beneath Lupita's bed told the grandmother what she had to do.

Since she was too old to drive, the grandmother ordered Isabella to drive them to the Valley to have the girl cleansed. They left early the next morning before sunrise to beat the heat of high noon. The grandmother's old Buick had no air conditioning, and halfway through the trip the heat had already become unbearable, amplified by the miles of nothingness stretching around them. Isabella lit a cigarette, much to the grandmother's disapproval. Lupita begged her sister to stop the car so she could stretch awhile. The big Buick came to a stop at the side of the road and Lupita climbed out onto the dusty shoulder.

"I'll be right back, I just need to walk around a little," Lupita assured her grandmother. But the grandmother noticed something strange about her eyes—their black color had become three shades lighter and seemed to glow like two setting suns.

"¡Lupita! ¡Ven!" she cried.

"Por *favor*, abuelita."

Lupita's head felt swollen. A dark cloud brought one of those sudden summer drizzles. It cooled the air temporarily, and the moisture bubbled and fizzed on Lupita's hot skin. She turned back to look at the Buick. It seemed far away as she watched her grandmother climbing awkwardly from it. She loosened the knot of her hair, and it flew about her head like the rays of a black sun before disintegrating in her fingers. A cool tear of liquid metal slid down the side of her breast where her santos had been pinned. As Lupita began walking up the road, her hands unconsciously brushed at the pieces of her dress that were beginning to turn to ash, dissipating on the wind. The grandmother, falling onto the gravel, called out her granddaughter's name as she watched the girl become a pillar of flame up the road, white light, like the halo of La Virgen.

THE DEVIL
IN THE VALLEY

David Rice

"THERE'S TOO MUCH LIGHT FOR THE VIDEO RECORDER," CRISTINA said as she pulled the cloth over the windows that looked out over Gloria's beautiful flower garden.

Cristina stood behind the tripod and pressed the "record" button. "Mamá Gloria, Mom says that you saw the Devil here in Edcouch, aquí en El Rincón del Diablo."

Gloria didn't answer. She relied on her granddaughter's belief in the myth that the old had very poor senses. But Gloria's fine-tuned ears could hear murmurs, and her eyes could still thread a needle.

"Is it true?" Cristina continued.

Cristina had been told not to ask this question, but she was too much like her grandmother. Gloria looked at the electronic equipment surrounding her. Black boxes listening and watching so as not to miss a word, a sound or movement, gave Gloria a grave sense of immortality.

Gloria didn't have to search for memories as the young do. They have not had the years of feeling their consciousness gently submerging into the subconscious, where truth dreams and madness whispers.

"Ay, Dios, sí, I saw him burn down Santa Teresa, him and his demons, but it didn't do any good. Everybody in Edcouch from El Rincón del Diablo y el Barrio de la Nalgada built a church out of bricks. It was hard work, but at least we were working for God, and not for the packing shed." Gloria paused and closed her eyes so she could see inside herself.

I was born here in Edcouch in 1920, before it was a town. Your great-grandfather was one of the founders of the town. He cleared all the land, pulling out all the mesquite trees and laying down all the pipes for water, and he dug the canals too.

Me, my mother, and father used to plant flowers and trees around Santa Teresa when it was a little house. We prayed to God to watch over us and he did, pero the Devil lived here too and he had lots of help.

I started working in the packing shed when I was thirteen, but I didn't want to. I wanted to go to school. Edcouch built a new school in '33 and we tried to go there. Bueno, lo que pasó era que, when we got to the school the principal met us at the door and said the school was not built for us. Our parents told us we should work with them in the packing shed.

Mira, when the land was cleared, all around Edcouch, Elsa, La Villa, Monte Alto, pues bueno as far as a horse could walk, qué bárbaro, it was very good land; vegetables and fruit grew with such sweetness and color. The owners of the packing shed told us, "Only the best leaves the Rio Grande Valley and everything else stays."

Everybody in my family and everyone we knew worked for the packing shed. If brown hands were not picking vegetables or taking fruit off the trees, they were inspecting or boxing them up and driving them away to other towns. My father was a truck driver. He and my tío drove trucks filled with vegetables or fruits every morning except Sunday. At church we always lit velas for the truck drivers.

When I was eighteen years old I fell in love and married Enrique. He was a truck driver. He was a handsome man and strong. The women at the packing shed thought so too, pero, it was me he wanted. We were so young. I thought nothing would happen to us, that we would live forever, but my mother said, "Last night a strong, cold wind pushed open the doors to Santa Teresa and blew out all the velas."

When our son, Ernesto, turned four, Enrique took him on a trip. I told him not to take Ernesto, but Enrique said it would be good for his son to travel with his father and grandfather. "No más los hombres," he said as he made a fist and pounded his chest.

I still don't know how the accident happened. They never told us. It took a day for the company to bring them home. They brought them home in the back of a truck, covered by a black canvas. Era el primer día de la canícula, and when they pulled back the canvas and I saw my husband and son facing each other, I swear I saw Enrique take in a breath. That's when I knew everything breathes, even the dead. My mother said they had their mouths open because the dead like to talk. Even today, when it gets real hot and the wind blows, I feel my husband's and son's breath and every day I hear their voices.

I kept going to church with my mother, and we still lit velas, but I was mad at God. It was hard for me to kneel in church. I didn't listen to the priest anymore; I didn't believe him. He worked for the church and they told him what to say. He would never marry and have children. How could he know what it was like to lose a child? Y Santa Teresa only loved Jesus; she didn't know how to love the imperfect. Pues bueno, I stopped going to church.

I worked hard every day in the packing shed, sixteen hours a day. I'd walk home late, sometimes past midnight. I was told not to walk home by myself because the Devil might get me, but people didn't understand. There was nothing inside of me for God and nothing for the Devil either.

On my way home I'd walk by a cantina, El Gato Negro, and it looked like a fun place. It made me happy because there was always a band playing and I could hear the music before I reached it. Once I passed it, I could still hear the music from many blocks away. Some of the girls who used to work at the packing shed quit their jobs to work at El Gato. Men called them chulas, and women said any woman who worked there was estúpida. I didn't know what to think, but I knew they made more money than any of us, so who was the estúpida?

Some nights I would stop outside of El Gato Negro and listen. They said evil things went on in that cantina, but with all that laughing and music? It didn't sound like they were suffering. At the packing shed we never laughed.

One day I was standing by the conveyor belt that carried thousands of tomatoes and began to look around. Women with sweat dripping off their faces. No fans to cool us off, no water fountains for our thirst. I looked at a box of tomatoes and on it was written "Only the best leaves the valley." I had been there fourteen years and many of the women had been there longer, but none had left.

My eyes were tired and my feet were always hurting from standing all day. But the owners never looked tired. They smiled and patted each other on the back. The harder we worked, the happier they were.

I was in charge of the women and my job was to make sure they worked hard even if they were sick or pregnant, and for what? To make the owners rich. I had been there for years and still made the same money as when I started. So I walked off the line and stood in front of the switch that controlled the belt. I turned it off. The shed was so quiet. I started pointing at women asking them, "¿Cuántos años tienes aquí?" Many of them said ten years. I told them we deserved more money, but no one listened. One of the managers told everyone to get back to work and they did, except for Conchita.

She took a step forward and said in a loud voice, "Es la verdad." Conchita was a big woman, bigger than the women and most of the men. She walked up and stood next to me and I shouted, "No se dejen." The manager looked worried. He told everyone to get back to work or no one would get paid. Women started picking up tomatoes and men began lifting boxes.

The manager walked over to the switch and turned on the conveyor belt and gave me and Conchita an evil smile. I took off my apron and hat and threw them on the tomatoes. Conchita got real mad and threw her apron and hat on the ground and grabbed a tomato and threw it at the manager. He ducked and the tomato stained the wall. We laughed and walked out. And for the first time in my life I felt cool, fresh air in my chest.

It didn't take long for the town to hear what happened at the packing shed. Most people were happy and said they would have done the same if they didn't have a family to support. We were heroes. Not just in Edcouch, but all around. Sí, we did the right thing.

Two days after I quit, Riche and his brother José came to my house. It was a good thing my mother was not home because she would not have let them in. They were the owners of El Gato Negro. Riche and José had driven trucks with my father years before, but they carried more than vegetables.

They said they heard what I did at the packing shed and wanted me to work for them. Bueno, I needed a job, but I wasn't going to be a chula. They said they wanted me to be manager, in charge of everything. They told me I would make three times what I used to make and have my own room, then I thought of Conchita. I told them I would only take twice as much if they hired Conchita. They said no, and I told them how Conchita had stood next to me in the packing shed. They still said no and right at that moment who knocks on the door and walks right in like it's her house? Conchita.

Conchita looked down at them and frowned. She pulled back her big arms and raised her chest, then made her thick hands into fists the size of melons. "What do these men want?" she asked with her low voice. I smiled and said, "This is my friend Conchita." They hired us.

My mother was mad. She said no man would marry me if I worked there. When she said that it scared me, but she missed being loved and I didn't want love to find me. I knew that if love found me in a casa of chulas, then it would be true love.

Riche and José introduced us to the girls and they were very young. We had twelve girls and the oldest was eighteen, but they acted much older at night when the lights were low and their makeup was bright. The first night in El Gato we didn't sleep because the music and laughter kept going until we could hear roosters singing to their hens through the thin walls. During the day the girls played and made fun of the men. I learned so much about men through those young girls.

I became the older sister they had never had and Conchita was the understanding mother they had always needed. They didn't like me until I broke a broomstick on a man's head. It was a busy night because it was a full moon and then something got into this man who was with one of our prettiest girls, Rachel. He started hitting her. When I heard her screaming I ran up to her room and there was this fat naked man slapping her like she was an animal. I jumped on him, but he was possessed and threw me off like a doll. When I fell to the floor I saw a broom in the corner and grabbed it. I hit that cabrón over the head as hard as I could, breaking the stick in half. He got up, pero he didn't even know where he was. I pulled him by the hair on his head down the stairs and let him fall on his face. Everyone stopped and I said, "Nadie jode con mis chulas." Riche and José looked worried, but the naked man's friends started laughing and everyone started laughing. I don't know how long that man was on the floor, but I didn't care.

After two years, I learned that most men were cowards. They don't have the strength to make decisions. They complained about the long hours at the packing shed and the low pay, but they never did anything about it. They'd fight with each other like little boys and if they lost, they'd go home and hit their wives. They were even afraid to walk home alone at night because they said the Devil would get them. But once you are afraid, the Devil has won.

This was the time the packing shed owners began to hire braceros from Mexico. The owners made an agreement with the rich in Mexico to send two thousand men with strong arms to work. With more workers the owners didn't have to pay more money. No one said anything except Javier.

One night at El Gato, Javier told the workers to quit complaining. He said, "Cada día, lo mismo. All you do is cry like babies. Pero nunca hacen nada." The workers stopped and then I stood up. "No se dejen," I said. The men looked at each other and Pedro, the head truck driver, said there was nothing they could do. Javier told them that there's always something that can be done. Javier was young and I thought to myself that if my husband were alive, he would be like Javier.

The truck drivers started to meet once a week, and Javier and Pedro led the meetings and everyone agreed that they would stop driving the trucks. The drivers would go to work but wouldn't drive until the owners paid everybody more. They were excited, but some were afraid. Javier told them we had nothing to fear but fear itself.

Many things happened when Javier was here. My life meant more to me, but I didn't want to get too close. He would stay with me at El Gato and we talked until the sun came up. I would tell him to stay because if he walked home by himself, the Devil might get him, and he was safe with me.

El Gato was full of the truck drivers the night before they planned to stop driving. They even brought their wives and children. The women said if their husbands walked out, they would do the same. Javier was happy and Pedro was too, but he told everyone to go home and get some rest. Javier stood up and said, "No, let's stay. 'Drink and be merry, for tomorrow we may die.' " The men laughed, but Pedro still left.

That night I held him so close. Trying to take him all inside, he was like a cloud or a feather. So light that he floated in my arms. Sometimes when I'm in bed, I feel like I'm floating. That's when I know I'm in his arms.

The next day me and Conchita walked to the packing shed to cheer for the men and women. It was a very cold morning and the beginning of the freeze of '51. Everyone was there, but they weren't doing anything. The manager was outside with Pedro next to him and he told everyone to get back to work. But no one moved. Pedro told them in Spanish to get back to work. One of the men said they were waiting for Javier. The manager adjusted his cowboy hat and spit chewing tobacco on the ground and said, "Javier is gone." The men and women lowered their heads and walked into the packing shed.

¡Qué coraje! I screamed and grabbed the manager by the shirt and started scratching his face. Then Conchita pushed me out of the way and hit the manager right in the face. Pedro tried to get Conchita off, but some men grabbed him. She kept on hitting the manager. The other managers came outside and it took four of them to get Conchita and me off the manager. Everybody was shouting and the manager had blood all over his face.

"You attacked the manager?" Cristina said with surprise.

"Pues sí. I knew that cabrón had done something to Javier."

Gloria leaned forward in her chair. "And three days later was when I saw the Devil burn down the church."

"So you really saw him?"

"Pues sí," Gloria said with a nod. "And not just him, but his demons. Burning the church down."

"Did he have horns, like they say he does?"

"Oh, yes. He had horns on his head, like a goat," Gloria said.

"And did he have a tail?"

"Pues sí. He even had chicken feet," Gloria said. "His eyes were red and his teeth so white. And he smelled so bad. Como caca y chi."

Cristina laughed, "¿Como caca y chi?"

Gloria put her hand to her chest. "Pues sí, mi'jita. You don't think the Devil is going to smell good, do you?"

Cristina nodded and grinned. "Did he have skin like a snake? And was it red?"

Gloria took in a breath and her smile faded. "Ay, mi'jita. Yes, he had skin like a snake." She paused and let her breath out gently with a sigh, and looked at the floor and caressed her rosary. She looked into the naïve eyes of the young child.

"Pero his skin is not red, it's white."

BAD DEBTS AND VINDICTIVE WOMEN

Stephanie R. Reyes

1

THIS IS A TRUE STORY. EXCEPT FOR THE WAY JUDY PENA TOLD IT TO me at my house at J.R.'s birthday party. So I am going to tell you my version of the story, the new and improved version that's full of wealth, greed, and the price you pay for selling your soul to the wrong broad. Not that there's a right person to sell your soul to, but the way lawyers are popping up in the Valley, you know someone's selling something to the right person. The story takes place at the Toluca Ranch, which is just outside of Progresso, along the Rio Grande. The main character of the story is S.F., this guy we went to high school with. I am using initials only on account that I want to protect the innocent, and plus, my boss Melo is attorney to one of the parties involved in this tale. Anyway. S.F.'s family had founded the ranch in the 1880s, and when his dad bought the farm, S.F. got the ranch, the money, and the ugly white Cadillac with the longhorn hood ornament, like the one Boss Hogg had on *The Dukes of Hazard.* Or was it like J.R.'s on *Dallas*? Anyway, this guy was something else. When he wasn't strutting his bony ass in his could-stand-up-and-walk-on-their-own Wranglers and in his ostrich-skinned, high-heeled boots—like the ones the artist formerly known as Prince wears—into Bocaccio's, the Jet-Set, or Sam's Club (it's a club in Reynosa, not the wholesale Wal-Mart club pendejos), he was with one of the bony-assed, ex-varsity cheerleaders turned sorority poster girls for domestic servitude in return for cosmetic surgeries and vacations in Acapulco, at the Tower Club or the Roundup. S.F. was a real lady-killer; actually, he never *killed* anybody, he just forced himself on them. Which is why telling you this story, my new and improved way, is so much more interesting than stupid Judy's old-school, rancho tale.

So it turns out that S.F.'s dad, M.F., had died of a bad case of cholera. He had taken his girlfriend to a restaurant in Matamoros, gotten some oysters on the half shell, and got a bad case of the runs. Who knew? S.F.'s mom had died when he was little and his two older brothers were just as bony assed and just as stupid. So when inheritance time came around, S.F. talked F.F. and P.F. into letting him control their share of the wealth, on account that he had taken some business class at the junior college in Kansas he played baseball at. Introduction to Business 1310 does not a Trump make. But like I said, they're dumb. So S.F. got the ranch—an old antique two-story house, the store that his brothers ran, 17 miles of virgin mesquite, and monte. But it wasn't enough. Despite the 5.8 million Gs that old M.F. left his son, he still wanted more. I think he was into coke at the time and was looking to score big money to buy big time.

2

"Can I speak to Mr. Villejo? This is S.F. calling."

"Yes, sir," said his secretary, "just one minute."

"Well, hey there, S.F., this is el Villejo. What can I do you for?"

Now this man was the lowest of the low. He was a full-blooded Mexican, ass as dark as mine, yet he spoke with an incessant country twang that ran together with his thick English accent. He said he picked up the twang when he was in the service, stationed in Altus, Oklahoma, during Korea. My suspicion is that Okies would be insulted by the nasty accent of his. Anyway. His name was Chemo Villejo, but his friends called him Chas Villejo, pronounced "viay-ho." He owned a loan company downtown and had been friends with M.F. for years. M.F. helped Chas set up shop, and Chas ran the books for M.F. The man's hair was jet black, courtesy of la Ms. Clairol, 'cause my cousin Melie worked at Curl Up and Dye, where he got it done, and he wore a collection of gold chains that made Mark Spitz look like a loser. Sansabelts of polyester, shirts by Arrow, boots by Rio's of Mercedes, of course, and a nice black Mercedes with limo tint.

"Well, Villejo, I need a way to make some money."

"Whatchu mean? You got almost 6 mill in the bank. The interest alone should be enough for you to live off of."

"Yeah, it's a lot of money, but well, you can never be too rich." And S.F. really believed that.

"It's that little piece of tail I've seen you aroun' town with. What's her name, Jov—"

"Her name is Jody, and I've dumped that tramp. Look, old man, can you help me find a way to make some more money or not? There's nothing wrong with wanting to expand the wealth. Now can you help me or not?"

Villejo thought about it for a while. Yes, he knew someone who could give S.F. the kind of backing he needed to make some money, but why the hell should he? S.F. was nothing to him, just the M.F.'s kid—and that's who his real allegiance was to. M.F. was a good man, worked hard. S.F. was just a dumb-ass punk in nice clothes.

"Goddammit, look, Villejo, if you can't recommend me to some-one, then I will take my business somewhere else."

"Hijo de tu madre, si supieras cómo te voy a chingar." This was the only time that Chas ever spoke Spanish. "Huerco pendejo, all right, yes, I'm gonna help you. Let me call over to the Des Gracias in La Feria. When you get there, ask for Evilina." Villejo made a call, called S.F. back with directions and S.F. was on his way. Villejo knew in the back of his mind that the Des Gracia family collected high interest on all of their investments. But, well, the kid asked for it, and against his best judgment, Villejo complied. I think it was the 15% finder's fee that S.F. promised that swayed the vote.

3

When S.F. arrived at the Des Gracia home, he was amazed at how beautiful it was. Some Oblate missionaries had built the house during the Mexican revolution because the family helped finance a new church in nearby Larampago. The Des Gracia jefe was a rancher, like M.F., but he didn't like ese sonofabiche on account that the jefe had liked one of M.F.'s sisters when he was younger, and M.F. threatened to kill him 'cause he didn't want his sister "with no damn Mex'kin who would take advantage." Little did M.F. know that his sisters were not the kind you needed to ask twice—si tú sabes qué te estoy diciendo. But the jefe had died and left the old limestone two-story house to his wife and only child, a daughter. They only had one child because his wife had narrow hips that she believed she inherited from the Spanish side of her family. In my experience, I've never met anyone who speaks Spanish with narrow hips. Anyway, so the ranch was sold off, and his widow Nina took off to Europe to see the world. His daughter, Evilina, stayed behind.

She was just happier at home "near the ocean, by the river." Well, that's the bullshit reason she gave, but I think it's really because the grieving widow had taken a young Brazilian guy named Paolo with her to explore the European continent—so he could help her grieve. I don't know about that. One time I was at the Des Gracia house for a barbecue, and I needed to go to the bathroom, so I went upstairs and I heard crying coming from the master bedroom, but it didn't sound like tears of sorrow. At least not in my experience. So Evilina lived alone, with the exception of Cata, their housekeeper, who stayed with her during the week.

Evilina was about 26, a few years younger than S.F., 'cause they went to high school together. She had gone to UT, was educated, and had never been pregnant or married. I think it's those three factors that automatically disqualified her as a viable, datable woman to men in the Valley. I mean she was smarter than most of those idiots, and she also carried less baggage. A lot of people thought she was a lesbian because she never dated men, but it's just that she never found one she liked. Excuse her for wanting quality, right? Anyway, she had dated some football player at UT all four years of college, then he turned pro and his back on her for some model from Norway or Iceland, one of those pelo miado countries. So Evilina came home.

4

Evilina opened the door 'cause it was a Saturday morning and Cata was gone. When she laid eyes on S.F., somehow his skinny ass and high-heeled boots managed to start a fire in her that the other pendejo had stomped out. She was in love. His face, his green eyes, his receding hair-line covered by a Stetson, the fact that, in boots, he was about her height—bien caballona at 5'9"—all of that did it for her. Go figure.

Of course the idiot didn't feel the same way. Sure, he thought she was attractive; he had never seen a Mexican chick that tall before. She had long brown hair like a white girl's and huge brown eyes. He could tell that she liked to tan, 'cause she had that "native" glow to her. He could also tell that she like to tan naked, 'cause he didn't see any tan lines coming out of that tube top or from under those hot pants. Nevertheless, S.F. only dated white chicks, despite the fact that they smelled like Band-Aids. He introduced himself and she asked him into the living room.

"Mr. Villejo said you were coming over. He said you need a loan to serve as capital for some investments. He gave me a brief run-through of your assets, and it looks like you've got the collateral for me to make you a substantial loan. I have to tell you, though, that if you don't pay off the loan in ten years, you will have to liquidate your assets, and your peace of mind will be mine." S.F. didn't know what the hell she was talking about. He didn't want a capital and he didn't want to liquefy anything. He wanted to be richer than he was and that was the end of that.

"So are you going to lend me the money or what?"

"Yes, I'm going to lend you the money, but I hope you heard what I said."

"Yeah, yeah, I heard you." He saw her start to write a check for an amount I am not allowed to disclose, on the fact that I work for the lawyer that handles her finances and I could lose my job, but it was enough to send a couple valley football teams out of state to play a game in Hawaii.

"Ten years," she said. "That's all that you've got."

"Ten months," he said. "That's all that I'll need."

5

Man, was that S.F. really stupid! In ten months, he had lost the quarter of a million that she had lent him at the cockfights and the bullfights and just fistfights in Reynosa. Plus, that idiot brother of his, F.F., had taken about two million dollars from their account and split to Aruba with some Mexican national that he had met while they were in the locker room of the athletic club. I know, it was a big shock for all of us, too. His other brother P.F. got a job in Mission as a citrus broker, but when he ran it into the ground, he took out an I.O.U. from their account, about 1.5 million, to save the business, but he just got ripped off because the business he worked for was a money laundering scheme for some Mafioso guy from Bishop or Driscoll. It is so true that "stupid is as stupid does."

So S.F. had to run the store, because P.F. was living with a stripper in Edinburg, and he was so messed up on coke or weed or acid all the time that he couldn't find his ass to wipe it, much less find his way to the store out there in B.F. Progresso. The truth is that S.F. didn't know shit about business or money; all he knew was how to spend it. So when la Jody, the ex-cheerleader sorority liposuctioned poster girl came to town after her divorce, S.F. spent his money on her. All of it. So that's how it went, and before he knew it, all he had was the house and the land, and his ten-year time limit closing in on him.

6

One day, S.F. was sitting out front in the Cadillac, which by that time only had one side of the hood ornament on it, when he felt this funny feeling. At first he thought he was just horny, which was the only other kind of "feeling" he ever had. But before he knew it, he was at the Handy Dan buying a cement mixer, a ladder, two-by-sixes, and wooden shingles. He got home that day and began to make a rock wall. It was about

20 feet long and 20 feet high. Then he made another parallel wall of the same dimension, about 10 feet away. He used the two-by-sixes for the roof, then he covered it with shingles. At the end of six months, laboring day and night, he realized that he had built a church. Then one day while he was putting up the door to the church, Evilina showed up.

"It's been ten years," she yelled over the racket of the hammer, "I came to collect my loan."

"What? I can't hear you; I'm hammering," S.F. replied. "Come closer." But she wouldn't come closer, and she wouldn't go inside the church. S.F. noticed this and walked inside the church to see if she would follow. She did not.

"Cool," he thought, "as long as I stay in the church, she won't be able to collect her money." So he told her that he would not be leaving the church anytime soon since he felt a need to meditate deeply and could she please leave, as she was distracting him from his metaphysical studies. Evilina gave him a look of hatred.

"All right," she said, "you go ahead and meditate, but I will get my money back, or your peace of mind will be mine." Well, the fire in her eyes scared him so much that he did you-know-what in his pants. Idiot. Anyway, once he saw her drive off, he made a mad dash for the house. He loaded up a bunch of clothes, utensils, a washbasin, soap, cookware, and canned goods into a wheelbarrow and hauled his ass back to the church. By sheer luck he had placed a water pump inside the church. Actually, I think he accidentally built around the damn thing and he hadn't even noticed. So there he stayed for ten years. Occasionally, P.F. and la Crystal Devine, the 42DDD headliner at the Showpalace, would stagger their rosy noses onto the property, and S.F. would send them out for food. But other than that, he mostly slept and watched TV, since he had had the insight to run a cable and extension cord from the house into the church. The guy was an idiot, but you gotta give him an "A" for thinking about the TV.

7

Well, a man can only go so long before his defenses get broken, and I think a man can go even less when he hasn't gotten laid in ten years. But a woman, a woman can go years, I mean *years,* and she will be just as pissed off and just as vindictive toward her victim as she was on day one. Evilina wrote the book. At the end of the ten-year stint of S.F.'s meditation, she came back. Actually, she moved into the damn ranch. First thing she did was disconnect the cable and the power that led from the house into the church. She knew that if no TV didn't surrender him, she didn't know what would. So day and night, she stood outside of the church waiting for S.F. to come out. Occasionally, he would peek his head out, and there she was, with a machete waiting to cut his head off. I mean, she wasn't always there. She would eat, sleep, and bathe, but he was too chickenshit to come out of the church, because he thought she was always there.

Eventually, Evilina had had enough. One night, she drove down to Fito's Mini Mart, filled up about five, five-gallon tanks of unleaded and drove her Bronco back to the Toluca. From inside the church, S.F. watched Evilina pour the gasoline around the perimeter of the church and light it on fire. OK, one thing they apparently did not teach the girl at UT was that rocks couldn't burn.

So she went back to Fito's, went back to the ranch and got a ladder. This time, the genius used the ladder to get on the roof and poured gas on the roof and in the windows. She wanted to burn S.F. to death. Apparently she too had seen the NBC repeat of *The Burning Bed.* Angered that Evilina was destroying the only thing he had ever built with his own hands—except for the reputation he had built for the way he used his hands—S.F. ran out of the church and started to wrestle with Evilina. Evilina managed to reach for the machete, and with one swoop cut his head off like the guillotine did Marie Antoinette's. "See," she said, "I told you that if you didn't pay me back in ten years, your peace of mind would be mine."

8

Actually, maybe I've been spelling "peace of mind" wrong this whole time. Maybe she said she wanted a "piece of his mind," meaning his head. Who knows. The only thing I am sure about is that the guy at Fito's got real suspicious of Evilina and called the cops on her. When she went back the second time, they followed her back to the Toluca, and they parked outside of the gates. They were within full view of what she was doing, but they didn't arrest her since there's no crime for setting fire to your own property, unless you claim it on your insurance. However, what they did see was S.F. charge at her and knock her down. When she killed him, they ruled it as self-defense. So that was the end of that. She sold what was left of the ranch, made her self a triple millionaire, and her ex and her got back together, on account that the leggy blonde, was well . . . blond. They got married and Nina and Paolo came, and well, they lived happily ever after. The end.

9

Wait! I forgot the moral of the story, since this is a cuento, and you know how we Mexicans like to use the shortcomings of others as material for jokes and lessons. So here it goes: Don't ever overestimate the passivity of a woman, 'cause you bargain with the wrong broad and you're bound to get burned. Or lose your head, at the very least.

BEYOND ETERNITY

Elva Treviño Hart

THE FIRST EVENING MARJORIE SPENT ALONE AT HER PARTIALLY renovated hacienda, a quiet descended on the countryside that she was not prepared for. No cars on the dirt road, no airplanes overhead, no dogs barking. Even the air didn't move. It was as if she were the only living being on earth.

That night she dreamed of peones dressed in coarse white cotton and guaraches, hundreds of them, working around the hacienda planting corn and herding livestock. She tried to speak to the ones working the mill, but they acted as if she were a spirit, invisible and silent. As she turned to go into the hacienda's kitchen door, a pregnant woman ran out screaming. When three shots exploded in Marjorie's ear, her eyes flew open. Instinctively, she threw back the covers and ran from the bedroom. At the door to the patio, she stopped. In the pale new light of the morning, she wasn't sure if the shots had been part of her dream, or if they had been real and brought her to waking consciousness.

Marjorie had been restoring luxurious homes her whole adult life. Now that she was retired, she was restoring her own, to live in until she died.

Ten years before, she and her husband had come to San Miguel de Allende for the first time to vacation and visit a friend. After their arrival in Mexico City, they drove north into the mountains for three hours. When they arrived in San Miguel, a feeling came over Marjorie that she couldn't explain. It was as if her very bones wanted to be there. She felt immediately at home with the people, the climate, and the town. She felt as if she could finally breathe a sigh of relief and never have to go anywhere again.

The next year, in San Miguel on vacation again, they bought a crumbling hacienda, which sat on forty hectares of land. The hacienda was not in San Miguel proper, but on the old road to the Sanctuary of Atotonilco.

But then her husband Horace died and her mother got Alzheimer's. During a seven-year absence from San Miguel, she had escaped from daily worries into books and dreams about the hacienda. She collected books in English and Spanish about the lives and homes of the hacendados of the previous two hundred years. She lived with her insomnia by listening to thousands of hours of Spanish tapes. She read books in Spanish with a Spanish/English dictionary by her side. She read Neruda and García Lorca's poetry into a microphone and then corrected herself. By the time she was ready to move to Mexico, Marjorie was reading complete novels in Spanish.

Thousands of times she imagined herself in the large courtyard of the hacienda. The purple, red, and pink bougainvillea colors would cascade over the wall, the scent of jacaranda would fill her nose, and the brilliant blue peafowl she intended to have would wake her in the early dawn with their long, mournful screams. Her daydreams and her night dreams woke feelings in Marjorie that she had never had. But the feelings stayed inside of her, waiting to be expressed when she was finally at the hacienda.

For the first few months after she moved to San Miguel, she couldn't live at the hacienda. There was too much basic work to be done like plumbing, electrical wiring, and roof repairs. When the bedroom, bathroom, courtyard, and part of the kitchen were finished, she moved in.

When she installed the first furniture, she invited her artist friend, Betty, to come and see the work in progress. "And where will the maid sleep?" Betty asked.

"Oh, Betty, I've never had a servant. I'll get gardening help later, but not a maid."

"Marjorie, a maid is absolutely necessary here. They know where and how to shop for all kinds of things you'll need. And they are best at dealing with the vendors. Especially with as much work as you've taken on with restoring this hacienda, you will need someone to cook for you. It's not like you can get take-out here on the old road to Atotonilco." Betty convinced her. Marjorie went to town and put an ad in the paper.

That night another dream shocked her awake. She was being made love to in the blue bedroom of her hacienda. But it was lovemaking like she had never experienced. Wild, passionate, and loud. The sexual energy in the bedroom swirled, rose, and dipped, carrying her with it. She awoke drenched with sweat dripping between her legs, and was more aroused than she had ever been in the fifty-five years of her life.

Horace had been a gentle, considerate, and patient lover. She felt she was somehow betraying him by having a dream like that.

A week later, she was wondering why no one had answered her ad when her friend Betty called. "Marjorie, my maid says that no one will work for you, at least not at night. She says your place is haunted. That's why it was empty for so long."

"Haunted! What do you mean?"

"Apparently it's become the stuff of legend all through these parts, at least among the Mexicans. Adelita, the kitchen maid of the hacienda, was the paramour of the hacendado. When her husband came back from a trip and found out she was pregnant, he killed her. My maid says the local mariachis sing a heart-wrenching song about Adelita."

"How did he kill her, Betty?" Marjorie forced herself to ask.

"He shot her—three times through the heart."

Marjorie got in her car and went to find her realtor. "What can I do for you, Mrs. Rawlins?" he asked. "How is that hacienda coming along?"

"Very well, except for the spirits."

"Oh, Marjorie, I knew you'd hear those old stories eventually, but that's what they are . . . old stories. Mexican superstitions. Norte Americanos don't believe that stuff."

"Yeah, well apparently all the maids in San Miguel do. I can't get a single one to answer my ad for work."

"Is that the problem? Well, no problem. I'll find you someone who's not afraid of old tales. Just give me a day or two."

"One other thing, Roberto. Who exactly did I buy my hacienda from?"

"Macías de los Santos, of course, like it says in the papers."

"Yes, I know, but who is he and how did he come to own the property?"

"He's a businessman in Mexico City, and he's the grandson of Hernán de los Santos, who is buried on your property."

"Buried there! You didn't tell me anyone was buried there!"

"It's only a few graves on the far northwest corner. All overgrown by now, probably. Most of the old haciendas have small graveyards somewhere on the property. You were in such a hurry to buy, we just didn't have time to discuss those things."

Marjorie asked for Macías de los Santos's address and phone number in Mexico City and left the office. The next day she bought a horse and complete tack for it. She didn't shop much, just trusted the owner of Rancho La Loma to sell her a mount to explore the countryside. She bought a grand, mature mare named Princesa.

The cemetery was not hard to find. There were two wrought-iron enclosures.

In the first, hidden by cacti and bushes, were three gravestones she could read. One was labeled FELICITAS BARRERA DE LOS SANTOS. She had died at sixteen. The other two were a husband and wife with the last name of Potrero. They had died in their late twenties. There were other headstones in the enclosure, but they were broken, and time and the elements had erased them almost completely.

In the other enclosure was an elaborate marble headstone guarded by a kneeling Jesús, La Virgen de Guadalupe, and two angels. It was Adelita. Next to her, placed there almost as an afterthought, it seemed, was Hernán de los Santos. The two lovers were alone in the enclosure.

There were fresh flowers on Adelita's grave. And not just one bunch, but three. The entire enclosure was weeded and brushed clean, as if by a labor of love. Someone obviously still cared about Adelita, fifty years after her death.

That afternoon Marjorie called Mexico City. When a maid answered, Marjorie asked for Señor Macías de los Santos in Spanish. "¿Bueno?" he asked.

"My name is Marjorie Rawlins. I bought your hacienda."

After the briefest hesitation, he said, "Yes, Mrs. Rawlins. How may I be of service?" It was her turn to hesitate. He spoke English and his accent was . . . British.

"Señor de los Santos, as you probably know, I'm working on restoring the hacienda to the way it looked one hundred years or so ago, and I was hoping you could answer some questions."

"Oh, I don't think so, Mrs. Rawlins. After all, it's almost fifty years since I lived there. I was very young when I left. I'm so sorry, but I just don't believe I can help you."

She switched to her best professional voice that she had used with reluctant clients. "Señor de los Santos, I'll have to tell you the truth. I've had several dreams. One concerned a young pregnant woman who was shot three times. I can't get a maid to work for me because they say the house is haunted. Adelita's grave is covered with fresh flowers. As you can see, there are a lot of unanswered questions, and I need your help."

Long pause this time, then, "Yes, I see."

"I intend to stay here, Señor de los Santos, spirits or not. It's my home and I've grown to love it in the short time I've been here. But in order to learn to live with the spirits, the dreams, and the fresh flowers, I need some history and some answers. The workers don't work on Sunday. Can you come then?"

After another pause, not so long this time, he said, "Yes, of course I will. After siesta if that will be all right."

"That would be lovely. Do you ride? I can arrange to have a mount ready for you. We could ride to the cemetery together."

❦╾═╾═╾❦

Señor de los Santos was delivered to Marjorie's door by a chauffeur in a gleaming new car. When he got out of the car, a wave of arousal swept through her like a sudden storm. There were the lips that had kissed her everywhere in her blue bedroom dream, there was the full head of silver-and-black curly hair that she had sunk her face into.

"Señora Rawlins?"

I dreamed you up before you arrived, she wanted to say. Instead, in a shaky voice, she said, "Bienvenido, Señor de los Santos."

The new maid had laid out a merienda for them in the courtyard under the jacaranda trees. Marjorie invited him to sit and served him coffee with shaking hands.

"I never thought I would be sitting here again. Thank you for inviting me."

"I needed to know, Señor de los Santos. I can feel things here and see things, but I needed to know the true story."

"Yes. Please call me Macías. I'll start with my grandfather, since he was the last de los Santos to live in this house. In my mind, every stone and tree on this property is filled with memories of him. He was born on this hacienda, as I was. But unlike me, he spent his whole life here. He was twenty-one when his father arranged a marriage for him with a girl of fifteen. It was common then for girls to be extremely young when they married. She died ten months later in childbirth. My mother was given to a wet nurse who was to feed and care for her. My mother was also mar-

ried at a young age. She and my father lived here on the hacienda, where
I was born. My grandfather took me riding all through these hills. I used
to think of him as an old man, but he was only forty when I was born."

Marjorie raised her coffee cup, finally calm enough to lift it without shaking.

He went on. "When I was a young boy of seven, my grandfather
fell in love with the kitchen maid, Adelita. Now stories abound in
Mexico of the patrón taking advantage of an unfortunate kitchen maid,
but this was not like that, no, Señora. Adelita was the brightest spirit I
had ever seen. She laughed gaily and sang passionately through her days
in the kitchen. She was the picture of health, with round breasts and
thick braids wound up with fat red ribbons. I hope I don't offend you,
Señora, by speaking so plainly."

"Please continue," Marjorie smiled, truly calm now. "And call me
Marjorie."

"Adelita's husband could not give her children. He had almost died
of a disease as an adolescent—mumps I think—and the disease had left
him sterile. Her father had married her off to this man, also in an
arranged marriage, when she was very young. It was not a happy marriage. Adelita's happiest hours were spent in the hacienda kitchen and
in the kitchen garden. From there, she mothered us all and made us
laugh. Especially my grandfather. She could light up his face like fire-
crackers on the Sixteenth of September."

He looked at Marjorie to see if she knew that the Sixteenth of
September was Mexican Independence Day. When he saw she did, he
continued.

"And Adelita liked to do it. I think it made her feel powerful to
make the patrón's sad face happily alive again. They fell in love. When
her husband was gone for days at a time with the business of the livestock of the hacienda, Adelita would disappear into my grandfather's
room. My grandfather knew this couldn't continue and he planned to
make some sort of arrangement with Adelita's husband—financial
probably—but he never got a chance. Adelita's husband came home
unexpectedly after being gone for months. By then her pregnancy was
clear for all the world to see. Her husband shot her, just like in your

dream. He was caught and executed, but by then my grandfather's heart was in shreds. He never recovered." Macías's eyes clouded over, and he stopped speaking.

"And your parents?" Marjorie asked quietly after a while.

"They died three years later of cholera. That's when my grandfather sent me away to my padrino in Mexico City. There was too much sadness here for a small boy."

"And you never came back?"

"Only briefly after my grandfather died, to pay my respects. I should have come back again, as I had some unfinished business, but my heart just got too heavy every time I thought about it."

"Would you like to ride now out to the cemetery?"

The driver brought him a garment bag and Marjorie led him into her bedroom to change into riding clothes. She was very nervous about having him in what she felt was her inner sanctuary, but it was the only completely finished room in the house.

"Where does your British accent come from?" she asked once they were mounted.

"My padrino sent his son and me to boarding school in England soon after I arrived in Mexico City. From there I went on to Oxford and spent many years abroad. When my wife got sick, we came back to Mexico. That's when you bought my hacienda."

So there's a wife, Marjorie thought. "I hope your wife is well now?"

"No. Her illness has dragged on all this time. The cancer has eaten her from the inside out; only her shell is left now."

"I'm so sorry. If I had known . . ."

"No, don't worry. She doesn't want me near her much anymore. Says I make her tired. She has two Mexican xoloitzcuintle dogs that are her best friends and constant companions. I believe she stays alive only for them."

They rode on in silence, letting the horses choose their own pace.

"Why are there fresh flowers on Adelita's grave?" Marjorie asked finally.

"It was terrible news in this whole valley when Adelita was killed. And my grandfather's grief at losing her became legendary. So when a young girl hoped for love like that of my grandfather's for Adelita, she brought flowers to Adelita's grave, hoping that Adelita would intercede for her from the other world. Legends like that live on for a long time in Mexico. I suspect it's young girls hoping for big love that are still bringing flowers to her grave. And the grandmothers, who were young when the actual events happened, probably encourage them."

They got to the cemetery and tied their horses to the wrought-iron fence.

"It's time to tell you about my unfinished business here. When I was about to leave the hacienda for Mexico City, my grandfather brought me out here to the cemetery. We stood right here where you and I are standing. He knelt on one knee so that he could look at me eye to eye. He said, 'Hijo, you are the only person in this world that carries my blood, so I am going to ask you to do something for me.' He sighed deeply and continued. 'You know how much I loved Adelita, and how much I love her still. I don't know how much more life God will grant me. I hope not much, because each day without Adelita is a penance. But only God knows. When I die, people will want to put my bones at my wife's side. I want you to tell them not to. And what you say will have to be, because you are the sole heir of this hacienda. I want my bones to be by what I most love. I want to be buried by Adelita.' I was terrified by the heavy responsibility he was placing on me. And I had no confidence that anyone would listen to me when he died."

Macías paced back and forth as he unburdened himself. Then he stopped, looked at Marjorie, reached into his pocket, and continued. "My grandfather wasn't done. He reached into his pocket, just as I am doing and produced this little leather bag. He said, 'In this little bag are the three bullets that killed Adelita. The doctor tore them out of her heart as I asked him to. When I die, I want to take these bullets with me. They will, I believe, tie my heart to Adelita's for all eternity. I am asking you, hijo, to promise me that you make sure they go with me when I die. I want you, with your own hand, to put them in the breast pocket of my death suit. Will you promise?' Sí, Abuelo, I answered, because I knew there was no other answer."

"But you didn't do it," Marjorie said.

"No, as you can see, I didn't do it. I was a young adolescent in an English boarding school. He died in his sleep with a note pinned to his chest. The note said, 'Bury me next to Adelita.' For all I know, he pinned that note to his chest every night. By the time I came back to pay my respects, my padrino had buried him as you see here. I had never told anyone of my promise, or of my failure to keep it, until today."

"Well, you'd better get busy."

"What do you mean?"

"I mean they're still here, wandering around, being miserable. I hear a man sighing and a woman crying. When I look, there's no one there. They ride in and out of my dreams at will. The room I chose as my bedroom was your grandfather's. Am I right?"

"Yes, you are right." Macías drew a large pocket knife out of his pocket, squatted next to Hernán's grave and started to dig in the dirt. When he had managed a foot or so, he emptied the bag into the hole. He covered the bullets, smoothed the dirt, and then took a few flowers from Adelita's grave and laid them over the disturbed earth.

"There," he said. "They are not in his pocket, but they are within reach. I should never have waited so long. Macías brushed off his hands and blessed himself with the sign of the cross. Then he made a sign of the cross over the grave. When he turned to Marjorie, his eyes were glistening with tears. "Are you ready to ride back?"

※┼━━━┼※

Several stars had appeared by the time they got back to the hacienda. "Would you like to have dinner with me in town?" he asked. "I've told you all about the hacienda, but I don't know much about you. I would like to get to know you better."

"Do you have a picture of Adelita?" Marjorie asked when they sat down to dinner at El Campanario, the restaurant across the street from the bell tower of the church.

"For an ofrenda?" he asked.

"A what?"

"Forgive me, I was thinking like a Mexican, and I assumed you were also. The Day of the Dead is a week from Monday. I thought you wanted to make an ofrenda to Adelita to see if the spirits would leave you alone."

"But I don't want to be left alone! Adelita and Hernán are the most exciting people I've ever had in my life! Things are never dull at the hacienda. The workmen move a load of bricks, and when they turn around, the bricks are somewhere else. My friends in the United States would never believe me, but I feel I live in a world half magical, half real."

"Then if you want to continue down this mad road, I will come back with portraits of Adelita and my grandfather. If you choose to make an ofrenda, I will help you."

They walked in the Jardín after their meal. Then they rode out to the hacienda with the moon roof of his car open to the stars.

By night, all that week, the dreams assaulted Marjorie with a vengeance. Her sexual dreams were even more intense now that she knew the history of the hacienda and of the room where she slept. And she also knew Macías. She knew that he was meticulously clean and smelled faintly of spice. She felt she could eat him like some subtly flavored dessert, enjoying every spoonful.

She started bathing before bed every night, as if preparing for a lover. She lay there waiting until the dreams took her like a wild river. Macías caressed her in Spanish and she could feel his hands on her, large, sure, and on fire. She awoke full of energy, filling her lungs with the morning air, which seemed to be fresh from God.

She gave instructions to the workers early in the day, then drove into town to the Biblioteca, where she read for hours about the Day of the Dead, poring over the pictures. The books said that the festival of the Day of the Dead was half pre-Columbian pagan and half religious. November first was All Saints Day and November second was All Souls Day. In between the two days, for an hour or so at midnight, the people believed that the veil between the worlds parted and the dead actually came back to earth to visit those they loved and to partake of the earthly foods and joys they missed. To honor the dead, and to make sure they enjoyed their brief sojourn back on earth, the living would put together an ofrenda for the dead person. These offerings looked like altars. They typically had a large picture of the person in their prime, plus a sampling of all the favorite foods of the deceased. If the deceased liked to drink tequila, lemonade, or hot chocolate, these were included also. The ofrendas ranged from the simple to the incredibly elaborate, with flower garlands, multicolored skulls made of sugar, and confetti.

Marjorie decided to prepare a base for their ofrenda. She bought a low pine table and had one of her artisans marbleize it with various shades of lavender and purple. She installed it in her bedroom between two windows, and covered it with a filmy lace tablecloth. She looked at many other things, but didn't buy them, as she wanted the building of the ofrenda to be a joint project between Macías and herself.

❦ ✦━━━✦ ❦

When Macías arrived, he told her he was staying at the Taboada Hot Springs, and asked if she would like to come and enjoy the hot springs with him.

She agreed, although she was nervous about appearing before him in a bathing suit. She was fifty-five years old, even though she had been feeling twenty-five lately. As nearly as she could calculate, Macías was very close to her age. But men liked younger women, and especially Mexican men, she thought. And besides, he was married.

But Macías looked only at her eyes while they sat in the warm water together.

"You make me want to do things I haven't done for years. I frequently rode to Taboada when I was a young boy. Of course the hotel wasn't here, but I loved to come here," he said. "Being with you makes me feel . . . younger."

"That's probably what your grandfather said when he fell in love with Adelita." The words were out of her mouth before she could think or take them back. She felt the color rising in her face and she looked away from him toward the trees.

"Perhaps. But these are my own feelings, right now, today." Feelings for you, she thought he might have finished, but he didn't. It was as if he wanted to make a clear distinction between the magic of the past and the reality of his feelings today.

❧+⊱━━⊰+❧

The next day they bought armfuls of fresh flowers at the market. The market was a riot of color as vendors had brought in truckloads of flowers for the Day of the Dead. Then they strolled through the stalls of the sugar figurine vendors and selected sugar sheep, sugar angels, and sugar skulls in various sizes and colors. Finally they bought a bag full of candles ranging in size from three inches to two feet. Marjorie had her new maid make chicken en mole, atole, tamales, and various other dishes that Macías told her Adelita would make for his grandfather. Everything was arranged by suppertime.

They ate a light meal in Marjorie's courtyard. Afterwards they lit all the candles of the ofrenda and sat on the floor at the foot of Marjorie's bed to appreciate their work.

"She looks like she was really full of life and love," Marjorie said as she looked at the portrait of Adelita.

"She was. My grandfather had that portrait painted the year after she died, from a small picture of her. Then he had his portrait painted to match hers, with the same background, the courtyard of the hacienda."

"Why didn't you ever come back?"

"There was nothing to come back for. Until now."

"I've never had a love like they had," Marjorie said, looking at the portraits.

He took her hand. "Neither have I," he said. The candles made the shadows dance in the room.

"I wonder how it started, their love affair, I mean," she said.

He turned her face to look at him. "Like this," he said and kissed her softly.

The room swirled and spun. Marjorie felt she was being pulled into a vortex from which she might never return.

❧+⊱━━⊰+❧

The next morning, while she lay next to Macías's still sleeping body, Marjorie wondered who exactly had made love to whom the night before. She had done mad, passionate things to Macías that she had never even thought of doing before. And besides, she had demanded to be pleasured in return. Macías had obliged her with the prowess of a virile man in his prime.

Was it Adelita and Hernán that had come when the veil parted between the worlds, taken over their bodies, and made love in the flesh one last night?

She smiled and felt her smile all the way down to her toes. She had had the best night of her life. Her dreams had become reality, better than reality. She had reached heaven itself. She felt she could die in peace, having known pleasure like that.

They were shy with each other when Macías was leaving. He held her a long time.

"Marjorie, I don't know if I can come back . . ." "Shhh . . ." she said, smiling and putting a finger to his lips. "It was enough. And it would probably never be that good again."

"Maybe you're right," he said. "But I would love to die trying . . ."

❋╌═══╌❋

That afternoon, Marjorie rode Princesa out to Adelita's grave with a basket full of fresh flowers. Like all the other young girls who decorated Adelita's grave, she was hoping for a big love.

INOCENTE'S GETAWAY

Elena Díaz Björkquist

FOR THE THIRD DAY IN A ROW, INOCENTE MUÑOZ DROVE TO WORK in a stupor. The sun's glare on the pavement blinded him and sent a shooting pain into his skull. He shut his bleary eyes and felt his head throb to the rhythm of his racing heart. He wished he could go back to bed. His eyes fluttered open just in time to swerve around a scruffy dog in the middle of the road. Damn dogs, always getting in the way, he thought. Inocente rubbed the stubble on his chin and shook his head like a prizefighter trying not to go down after a punch to the jaw. Thanks to his stupid foreman, he had started drinking when he got home from work yesterday. On the way into the house Sukie, his dog, tripped him, so he kicked her. He didn't feel like eating dinner, so he drank instead. Later he slapped Soledad when she tried to take the bottle of tequila away from him. Maybe he punched her a couple of times. That part was fuzzy. Did he kick her too or did he dream that?

This morning Soledad and the kids were gone and the dog was dead. Every time he put the fear of God into Soledad, she ran home to Mamá Aguirre. This time they could stay there. See if he cared. He belched. For a moment he thought his breakfast was coming up. A six-pack of beer chased with a gurgle of tequila did not taste as good the second time around. Inocente swallowed hard and his heaving stomach settled for the moment.

He punched in to work twenty minutes late. He had only five more days to go before his two days off. They had to work twenty-six straight days before getting a miserly two days. T.D. must think they were super-men. This schedule was killing him. How did the other men do it? If he didn't have his beer and tequila, he'd never make it to his days off.

Where the hell was his truck, his Posita? Puffs of dirt exploded around him with each step. The sun sizzled his skin. By the time he reached the truck, sweat had soaked his denim work shirt at the neck, armpits, and back. Phew! He reeked and he knew it. When was the last time he'd showered? Who gave a damn? Inocente stumbled up to the huge dump truck, his truck. What a beauty! To everyone else it looked just like the others, but not to him. He loved this truck, his Posita. On the dashboard he had painted a posy with the name "Posita" printed underneath. His left arm sported a tattoo, a duplicate of the colorful painting on the dashboard.

Inocente climbed into the doorless cab and settled into the seat worn to the contours of his body. A satisfied sigh escaped his lips as the engine roared. What power! The truck rumbled a greeting, but only he could hear her words. "Good morning, Inocente! I'm here to do your bidding. Let's get to it."

He stroked the posy on the dashboard as if it were a kitten. The tattoo on his hand, a reminder of time served in la pinta, spelled out the word "love"; one letter for each finger. His other hand displayed the word "hate." When he was drunk, he wrestled one hand with the other to impress his kids. Most of the time, "hate" won.

"Hey, you up there. Inocente!" Herbert Johnson, the foreman, looked like a toad standing on the ground beside the truck. Inocente wished Johnson were in front of him. Then he could drive Posita over the fat gringo supervisor. Splat! He giggled at the thought and a rancid belch escaped his lips. The beer and tequila mixture in his stomach threatened to spill up his throat until he gulped it back.

"What 'cha want, Mister Johnson?" You turd-faced toad, he mumbled to himself.

"You're on level twenty-three today and no slacking off like yesterday. I don't want no complaints that you didn't do as many loads as the others."

"Yes, sir. I'm hopping to it!" Inocente tapped his aluminum hard hat in mock salute with the hand tattooed "hate." He gunned Posita's engine, leaving the foreman in the dust, shaking a fist at him. "Damn! Johnson's getting too big for his pantalones. One of these days, Posita, me and you'll bring him down to size."

He patted the posy on the dash. The truck lumbered along at a fast clip and soon caught up to another just like it. Inocente shifted down and braked. Damn it all to hell! These mojados drove like old ladies out for a Sunday drive. He reached under his seat and pulled out a bottle of tequila. Ah! Much better.

Inocente looked around the open pit mine as he drove down to his assigned level. In front of him, other big trucks queued up for loading. On the levels far below, the gray trucks looked like a convoy of ants going in two directions. Empty trucks headed one way and loaded ones in the other.

Bored, he reached for the bottle again and took another swig. Amber fluid dribbled down the sides of his mouth and Inocente wiped it away with his forearm. Damn that Soledad! She'd left him again, but this was it. A man could only take so much. Just wait until she tried to come back. He'd have a thing or two to say about that.

The gigantic shovel dumped a load of rock in the truck in front of Posita. Inocente maneuvered Posita to take its place, but parked her too close to the shovel. The shovel operator yelled at him but Inocente couldn't hear. The operator's signals were obvious, however, and Inocente backed Posita up and tried again. This time it was okay and he felt Posita lurch as tons of waste rock pounded into her bed.

"Pendejo operator! I'm sorry, Posita." Inocente's "love" hand stroked the dash. "One of these days I'm gonna get you away from this torture."

"Why not now?" The words came as he shifted gears. "Now! Now! Now!" Posita's jumbo tires sang as they crunched over the rocky road.

Inocente pressed hard on Posita's accelerator and felt a surge of speed in response. "Now! Now! Now!" Her song thrilled him.

"You're right, Posita! Why not now? I've had it with this pinche job and I'm tired of being tied down. Soledad was fun before she had those kids, but not anymore."

"Leave her!" Posita rumbled as Inocente backed her up to the edge of the dump to release her load of rock. "Let's get away!"

"Get away? Now?" Inocente shifted Posita's gears as he neared the road that led to the mine's entrance.

"Get away! Get away!" Posita's tires crooned and suddenly the steering wheel whirled in Inocente's hands. They raced toward freedom.

Inocente could not contain his excitement as Posita barreled down the road to the gate. He laughed and yelled, "Let's go, Posita!"

"Get away! Get away! Get away!" Posita sang an insistent song. The huge truck thundered past the guardhouse, missing Pete López by a hair only because he jumped out of the way. Inocente snickered at Pete sprawled face down on the roadside.

His "love" hand gripped one side of the steering wheel. His "hate" one, the other. What a ride! Inocente's excitement mounted. For three years, he and Posita had poked around the rocky pit roads. Each day he dreamed what it would be like to take her out on smooth asphalt.

"Get away! Get away!" Posita's tires murmured as they sped faster and faster down the hill and through Morenci. A two-tone green Chevy coming out of the parking lot in front of the T.D. Mercantile squealed to a stop as the big truck zoomed up to it. Posita crunched over the car's hood and demolished it.

"¡Cabrón! A Chevy's no match for my Posita." Inocente threw his head back and howled like a wolf.

A black dog attempted to cross the road under the pedestrian bridge between the two elementary school buildings. Splat! Through the rearview mirror, Inocente saw a dark stain where the dog had been. Too bad it wasn't Johnson, the foreman.

Down the hill sped Posita—past the high school, the football field, and through the tunnel. Inocente felt like a king sitting high on his throne. He and Posita owned the road. He steered her down the center of the road. Cars coming toward them jerked out of the way. Some crashed into the rocky bluffs on the side of the road and others drove into ditches, both options preferable to being squashed by Posita.

"This is power!" Inocente waved to his subjects as he drove past, yanking on Posita's air horn. Below the tunnel, Posita slowed to maneuver the curves before the smelter. When they hit the straightaway after the big curve in Plantsite, Inocente floored it. He felt invincible! Nothing could touch him while he drove Posita.

Down the mountain they thundered, Posita's tires humming on the paved road. "Get away! Get away!"

Inocente wished the old road to Clifton were still open. That would have been a fantastic ride with multiple switchback curves all the way. He geared down for the hairpin curve at the bottom of the mountain and pumped the brakes. Posita rounded the curve, tipping over to one side as if about to overturn, but regained her balance and sped on. They were on Highway 666 now.

"This is it, Posita. This is the road I've been telling you about, El Camino del Diablo."

Up ahead, Inocente saw a roadblock and the flashing lights of DPS patrol cars. The pinche guard must have called ahead. Inocente didn't brake. Uniformed men scattered out of the way seconds before Posita smashed through the barrier and over the cars. "Get away! Get away!" Posita's siren voice egged him forward.

In the rearview mirror, Inocente saw men scurrying to a couple of undamaged cars. The chase was on! Squealing sirens trailed him.

"Hot shit! Go, Posita! They'll never catch us. No more twenty-six days on, two days off! We're gonna be free! Go! Go! Go!"

Cars, people, and animals scooted out of Posita's way as she zipped through Clifton. The giant truck carried Inocente over the railroad tracks and onto the bridge. He thumbed his nose at shocked pedestrians; Posita's litany ringing in his ears, "Get away! Get away!"

The cop cars could chase them, but they couldn't stop them. No one was foolish enough to drive in front of a five-yard truck. Inocente chuckled as Posita climbed the hills outside Clifton. If a car got in front of them—tough luck!

The road leveled out and Inocente stomped on the accelerator. "Hot dog! We're unstoppable, baby!"

At the Three-Way Drive-In, Inocente steered Posita to the right toward Safford. They barreled down the hill to the narrow bridge over the Gila River. Panicked, he brought both feet down on the air brakes and realized he'd made a mistake. Posita's engine cut out. Damn it! The cardinal rule in driving a five-yard truck was to gear down and apply the brakes bit by bit. They were in for it now. No motor meant no brakes. Posita could not be stopped. As she went down the hill, she gathered speed. She flew onto the bridge and Inocente thought they were going to make it. But she was going too fast and before Inocente could change her direction, Posita bounced off the bridge railing. Inocente jerked her steering wheel in the opposite direction. Posita went into a long, slow skid and plowed through the opposite side of the bridge.

Inocente tumbled out of Posita's open doorway. His eyes locked on Posita as she plunged into the river below. Seconds later, he followed his beloved. The last thing he heard as he smashed into Posita's broken body was a whisper in the wind, "Get away! Get away!"

⚜ ╠═══╣ ⚜

Two patrol officers stood at the broken bridge railing and peered down at the wreckage in the shallow river below.

"What a mess! That guy must have flipped his lid." The cop made a circular motion at his right ear. "Plumb loco."

Two sleek black ravens flew up from the wreck. He could have sworn as they flew over him that their cawing sounded like "Get away! Get away!"

LILITH'S DANCE

Gary G. Hernández

As fear is outwardly inferior to love, so love is inwardly inferior to fear.

—PICUS DE MIRANDULA, *Conclusiones Philosophicæ,
Cabalistce et Theologiæ* (1486)

LEANING AGAINST A GRAFFITI-SCARRED COLUMN, I WAIT FOR MY train. I hear his shuffling feet, smell his sour odor.

"Yo, man, got a cigarette?" His voice has a quality which only years of cigarettes and substance abuse can achieve.

Taking a long drag, I glance away.

"Yo, man, you hear me?" His head bobs like a carsick dog. His voice grows louder and loses some of its coarseness. For an instant he almost sounds sober—almost.

"You got a cigarette?" he repeats.

"I'm out," I lie.

"Give me a drag, then."

"That ain't going to happen. Now beat it," I say in my best New York accent. Flicking my ashes, I look down the tunnel again. No lights. Shadows rustle against the walls: rats.

"Yo, man, give me a drag." He's whining now. For a second I think he might cry, but then he reaches out and grabs my coat. His hand is stark white, feminine, with long crimson nails. Lilith.

A familiar static hum starts in low, a soft itch at the bottom of my ears.

The platform is empty; the air still and quiet. I slip a hand under my coat to my belt and feel my knife. The sheathed edge tugs at my pubic hair as I unsnap the holster strap.

The static erupts into a crackling whirl. I know if I listen closely, I'll hear a legion of voices.

Stepping closer, the bum tightens his grip and whispers: "Man, I don't have nothin'. No money, no home. Gimme a drag, man."

He's close enough for me to count the pellets of snot tangled in his beard. Six.

"I'm homeless, you're homeless, we're all homeless," I say. "Nobody cares and I'm not giving you a drag, so get your hand off me."

He blinks once. He blinks again, and I poise the tip of my knife carefully in the center of his forehead.

"We ain't homeless," he agrees, dropping his hand and smiling nervously. "We live in New York City. New York's our home. Just look." He gestures slowly to the tunnels and piping.

"This is beautiful," he continues as he waves his delicate hands. "Beautiful. It's industrial art. These subways . . ." He looks at the ceiling as if he's noticed it for the first time. "This is *man-made;* we made this. This is our home."

His skin breaks. A small rivulet of blood runs down his nose, but he keeps talking, his raspy voice wavering in and out of audibility. The din of a thousand crying voices weaves into one tight scream as I swipe the knife down his face. His left cheek splits open so quickly it doesn't have time to bleed. Driving the blade into his gut, I wrench upwards, slitting his innards open like a sack of wet mulch. As I withdraw my knife, he drops to his knees and soundlessly slumps over his oozing guts.

His hands are still twitching as I hack them off. The metallic bee-hive in my ears slowly fades.

$+$

"Some believe in a great cosmic unity that links men, beasts, and even thought together in a single weave. For the most part it's New Age junkies looking to assuage the sting of their meaningless lives, but among them you can find a few otherwise rational and intelligent peo-ple. Life for them is a great mathematical equation. Like a balance sheet, every credit has its debit and in the end both reconcile to zero. For every good there is an evil in equal proportion." Her voice is com-forting and I relax in its embrace.

"Yin and yang and all that," I finally say.

Lilith nods then asks, "How's the salmon?" Her smooth, pale shoulders contrast sharply against her ebony evening gown and long black hair.

The restaurant is nice. I've never been here before, but Lilith high-ly recommended it. It's a dimly lit affair with a maritime motif. Black and gold. The atmosphere is soothing, cool.

"Fantastic," I reply. Taking a small forkful, I offer it to her. "Try it."

"No thanks." Leaning forward, she sips her burgundy wine with-out picking up the glass. "Fish and red wine don't mix."

I put my fork down and hold my glass up for a toast. "Here's to us."

"Us." Lilith smiles. Her eyes are dark—reflectionless. A car passes outside. Through the grimy window, the headlights look like weak flash-lights. I stare at the cracked window, looking for my reflection.

The night is cold.

The restaurant is gone. It was never there, of course. All night we've been tucked away in the cramped attic of my house. Just another one of Lilith's games to keep herself entertained, or me. I don't suppose it really matters. But Lilith is here. Lilith is forever here.

Clicking off the single overhead light, I sit back down in the dark. Even in the tight blackness, I see her eyes.

It always comes down to this, always something new as soon as the old is quenched. First it was the hands, touching me, caressing. Now it's the eyes, expressionless and black. More than the cold, the eyes chill me. They're so lonely, buried in the damp soil of despair. It hurts just to look into them—the same way it used to hurt when she touched me.

But I had wanted her touch then and I want her eyes now.

"You look tired," Lilith says.

"And you?"

Feigning a smile, Lilith brushes her hair back with her handless wrists.

§ ⊱───⊰ §

Catacombs run under New York City. They wind like veins, touching the subways here and there, creeping under sub-basements, twisting like madness. New York's a very big place and you have to put your dead somewhere.

I see them every day, the dead. Some have well-paying jobs, others are homeless. They cry to themselves and argue with shadows; they talk on cellular phones and eat sushi with their fingers.

As an assistant professor of English at NYU, I can't afford the high rent of the city. And even if I could, I'd still opt to stay across the river in Jersey where the houses are old and filled with dark urban memories.

Two years ago, almost to the day, I had a crisis with my work. After years of worshipping in the great halls of literature, I just couldn't face it anymore. I arrived in the City but, instead of stepping into my office at precisely 7:35 A.M. as I had every weekday morning for the past six years, I just kept walking.

I spent the morning in Washington Square Park, watching transvestites preach to invisible congregations and teenage dealers sell drugs to not-so-invisible children. I caught lunch in Chinatown, then wandered the galleries of Soho, pondering the meaning of art. That evening, on the way home, I murdered a homeless man.

Altogether, it was a full day out.

The act was neither quick nor clean; in fact, I puked my lovely Chinatown lunch all over my victim. The stink, the blood, the puke—

it was more than I could bear, but at the crux of it was something immensely pleasing, something that bore repeating again and again. The next day I went back to NYU and attacked my work with the vigor of a fresh grad student. I was revitalized, reborn. One week later I killed again.

Since then I have become an existential vampire of sorts—if I don't kill, I feel lost in the vacuity of my existence. Killing gives me a sense of purpose that Lacan and Derrida can never inspire.

I've killed countless people—and not all of them homeless. Some, I'm sure, had extravagant homes and wonderful lives.

And it generates spending money. Not a lot, but every little bit helps. After all, how much can an untenured assistant professor clear after city, state, and federal taxes? How many 101 composition classes do I have to teach just to keep out of polyester?

The scholarly life has its price. Publish or perish, they say. Well, there's more money to be made in the perishing business than people would think.

Above all, killing satisfies a deep-rooted longing. When I was a child, my greatest daydream involved a catastrophic event that eradicated all human life from the face of the earth. Their orderly, peculiar homes, however, remained.

I'd reverently investigate each home, opening the refrigerators to see what kind of leftovers they had. I'd drift through each room, breathing in the dust and bacteria. What kind of dishes were stacked in the sink? What was on their bookshelves? Homes are like Skinner boxes: cold pizza in the fridge and Chex Mix on the counter say more about a person than that person could say about himself.

It's the implications, the glorious implications, that thrill me. Killing people and sifting through their pockets is like living my childhood fantasy. Instead of houses, I explore people—my own fleshy, mute Skinner boxes.

And then there's Lilith. I can't remember exactly when she came into my life, but it was sometime after my first kill. She is the manifestation of pure love, sacrifice incarnate. Eons ago she renounced her divine station as the first wife of Adam for the principle of selfhood. There would be no bowing to man, nor to the father. There would be no God-serving fall and no off-the-rack plan of salvation. In ultimate defiance she cried the ineffable name of God and fled the garden before it became popular. And now she shares a house with me in a Jersey suburb. A little untidy, I must admit, but she's one hell of a lover.

❊ ╪➤═══╾╪ ❊

A frigid draft runs up my back as I shuffle my way free of the morning crowd. They're hurrying off to work, most of them already late.

Slowly, I trudge up the subway steps, refusing to touch the railings. Year after year the paint layers thicken, never covering the scars of dilapidation, but accentuating them more. The gouges and irregularities are like acne.

Rounding the corner, I face another flight. The sun glares off the snow at the top of the tunnel. Glancing back, I catch the furtive glance of an attractive woman tromping down the stairs. Probably works the graveyard shift somewhere. Probably heading home to her small but sensible apartment overlooking the river.

Our eyes lock—cold, dark, familiar. Lilith's eyes. I hear a far-off windswept ringing, a staticky rustling.

I smile to myself as she deftly drops a token into the slot with her too-well manicured nails. Her amply fed rear wiggles through the turnstile; she runs her fingers through her hair, tossing the already disarrayed tangle of red locks into greater chaos. I'm filled with yearning. My pants tighten as I quietly retrace my steps.

The maelstrom lets loose in my ears. I can't even hear her scream.

Three hours later, it's those same red locks which trouble me. They lay bunched up under one side of her severed head, causing it to sit lopsided on my desk. A liquid, which can't be blood and certainly isn't tears, seeps from the emptied eye sockets and collects in a pasty pool at the base of her neck.

My sock sticks to the small droplets on the floor as I recline in my chair. My stomach churns, but is filled and sated.

Lilith whispers in my ear. Her warm breath arouses me. I feel her cool breasts against my bare back. Tracing my cartilage, she licks my ear, tickling my lobe.

She whispers again. I can't tell what she's saying, but it's not important. It isn't the words, it's the breath—the absinthe of lust.

Turning my head, I kiss her hard, sucking her impossibly long tongue. She searches the crevices of my mouth like an eel in mud. I lean her backward onto the desk, knocking the bleeding head from its roost. It rolls like a beach ball half-filled with water, finally stopping as the nose wedges against the door.

Moistening her lips, Lilith speaks my name, enticing me further. Her voice is iced vodka, cool and intoxicating.

She can speak every language known to man and more. She speaks to me in the tongue of the dead, in the tongue of the living, in the tongue of my soul. I answer her in the only tongue I know.

She speaks on, staring blindly at the ceiling through blood-encrusted wells that once held her eyes.

❊╪══╪❊

Monday morning is no time to review a final thesis. Blair, my Wordsworth infected graduate student, sits opposite my desk fidgeting with an enormous stack of papers and several texts with multicolored markers erupting from the tops like Mardi Gras fanfare.

He whispers something.

"What?" I say, leaning forward. I squeeze my coffee cup tightly as a static hum begins to fill my ears.

Blair reads from the topmost paper. "What Lovecraft is suggesting is not only a departure from 'popular standards and values,' a step away from 'moral didacticism,' but a radical break from that which these uphold—an all-balancing center." His voice is breathy and insecure; I can hear every smack of his tongue.

"That's your thesis?" I ask. I'm distracted beyond reason. The static becomes a swirl of wispy songs, of disquieting cries. Blair looks up from his papers, perplexed.

"Well, yes. I want to explore Lovecraft from a Derridean angle, and I think this pretty much establishes it." His voice is like an anchor. I try to focus on it.

"That?" I say. I can hear my own voice far away. It's trembling with excitement and fear. Not here, I think, not at my office.

I push myself away from the desk and face the window. It overlooks nothing. Other professors have a view of Washington Square Park; I have a view of a dirty alleyway off a nameless street.

"That's pure unadulterated crap," I say. "You're going nowhere. Deconstruction is out, and who the hell is this Lovecraft anyway?" I can hear Blair's fat, pestilent tongue trying to form a response, but the static is rising.

"Look at me," a voice moist and unearthly says in perfect Latin.

I shake my head and focus on the glass. I can see Blair's reflection. It's just him, good plain English-speaking Blair—couldn't speak Latin if his doctorate depended on it.

I see his lips moving. "But the committee already accepted it," he's saying. "And you were part of that committee. I've researched this for six months now." His lips stop moving, but the words still come, this time in an Old English dialect: "I want you so bad. I need you so bad." It's Lilith's voice, soft and delicious despite the hard consonants and swallowed vowels.

I turn on my heels and step up to Blair, nose to nose. His eyes are welling with tears and he bites at his lips.

"I'm only going to say this once," I say. "I want you to get out of my office. I'm not playing this game. Not here, not now. Understood?"

Blair really is crying now. His breath comes in shallow staccatos. His lips quiver and he licks at them with his apink, wet muscle.

I head-butt him across the mouth. He falls hard against the closed door, blood spilling onto his neatly pressed shirt. My hands shake as I grab him by the hair and drive my knee into his face again and again. His nose collapses with the harsh crunch of cartilage.

The cries become sobs. Outside the door I can hear curious murmuring and small cries of alarm. Mouths and tongues everywhere, whispering, yapping, swallowing.

Digging my hands into Blair's mouth, I pry it open. For a moment Blair struggles, biting my fingers and pulling my arms. I slam an elbow into his shattered face. The resistance stops. The sobs become gurgles.

I pry at his mouth again. The door rattles, the murmurs now shouts.

Dropping to my knees, I fight for more leverage. With a crack, his jaw snaps and tears. I force my mouth not on but *in* Blair's. Tugging and sucking at his tongue, I bite it off at the base. The flesh tangles between my teeth. Sweet, bitter blood washes over my teeth and gums, dribbling down my neck.

The door finally opens. The rhythmic static in my ears recedes, replaced by the secretary's screams.

Lilith smiles, her delicate mouth bruised and swollen, tongueless.

MALDICIÓN

Guadalupe García Montaño

"Buenas tardes, Padre." Sofía walked by the church's front steps where Father Jacinto was busy sweeping away the day's dust.

"Dios te bendiga. Rumor has it you had quite a day en la delegación today." Father Jacinto kept up to date on the latest town gossip from his talks with the women who came by to help him clean the church. Out of all the women her age, Sofía had been the only one in town to actually have a job even after she got married. She did not help clean the church, but she made sure to take a few minutes to talk to the priest on her way home every afternoon.

"Sí, Padre. But one would have to be dead not to know that something was going to happen today. I mean, after all the commotion last night. With Don Refugio blasting away that old shotgun of his in the middle of la plaza. But it got straightened out today. No sooner had I typed up his declaración, than one of his peones comes running in yelling that Don Mauricio was going to shoot those damn cows in twenty minutes if Don Refugio didn't get them out of his fields. So they both ran out like the devil was after them." Sofía let out a laugh.

"So the cows weren't stolen at all?"

"No, Padre, and Don Refugio just made a fool of himself running crazy last night yelling that no one better be having his precious cows for dinner. Ay, those two riquillos are never going to stop hating each other."

"I'm glad you found something to lighten your day, hija. I know it has been tough for you lately. Is your daughter behaving herself yet?"

"Ay, Padre," Sofía's eyes lost their sparkle, "I don't know what to do with her anymore. Since Ricardo left for el Norte, Mariana's been bien rebelde. I understand she misses her papá, pero this is too much. Ya no me hace caso."

"No te deseperes, hija. Have patience and you'll see she'll come around with the Lord's help." Father Jacinto lifted a hand to Sofia's shoulder. "Ten fe."

"I don't know if faith is going to do it, Padre. I don't know what it will take to get her to leave those friends of hers. No le traen nada bueno, just a bunch of bad influences."

"Is she still going out with los hijos de los Zamora?"

"Sí, Padre, and I've told her over and over that those rich kids are no good. They're just lucky their papá gets them out of the trouble they get themselves into. Si lo sabré yo. I've seen those boys come in and out of la delegación since they were old enough to shoot un rifle. Pero, it's their sister, Marisol. She goes along with her brothers and then drags my Mariana with her."

Father Jacinto rested his hands on his broom. "Fuerza, hija. A firm hand is all she needs."

The midsummer sun was hanging low on the horizon, making Sofía's shadow grow long from under her feet. She looked down the dusty road, thinking of the many times she had heard the priest's advice. "Maybe, Padre, maybe. I hope so. I spend so much time being angry at her. I'm afraid que uno de estos días, I'm going to do something horrible to her." She glanced west at the sun. "Bueno, Padre, I want to get home before it gets dark."

Sofía reached for the priest's hand, kissed it gently, and set out on the long walk home. She remembered Mariana's childhood. It was all so different when they were a complete family. Ricardo treated Mariana like his little princess and the three of them were happy together. He and Sofía had grown up in humble homes, so, when they were both working and got married, they decided their children would never want for anything. "Todo pa' mis hijos," Ricardo would say as he held his ear to Sofía's belly in the weeks before Mariana was born and then as he held her in his arms in her first years. Sofía often worried that he was spoiling her, but the joy she saw in both their eyes kept her quiet all those years.

Then a new land reform law came along and, in the government's efforts to help the poor, it got rid of many jobs in the region. The new law took land away from the hacendados and gave it to peasants in the area. For Ricardo and Sofía, it was a mixed blessing. They received a small parcel of land on which they built their home, but Ricardo had been the capataz for the Hacienda Las Mariposas. When the government drove out the owner, Ricardo lost his job. Y de ahí, pa'l real, thought Sofía. They could no longer afford to buy Mariana everything she wanted. The girl's attitude toward her father changed dramatically. She no longer wanted to go to la plaza with him since he did not buy her the helados and trinkets she was accustomed to. And when Ricardo left for the United States, Mariana let loose all her anger on her mother.

Ricardo had been gone for three years and, while the money he sent was enough to live well, Sofía wished he were home to help her raise their daughter. Paciencia, she thought as she reached her home.

As she stepped in, she heard Mariana singing in her bedroom. She headed for the back of the house. "Hija, I'm home."

Mariana stood in front of her dresser mirror wearing a blue dress. In one hand she held a hairbrush, while the other was busy adjusting a lock of dark hair behind her ear. "Hola, Ma. I'm going out tonight."

Sofía leaned against the door frame and crossed her arms in front of her chest. "No, hija. I don't like you going out every weekend. Y luego con los Zamora. Mariana, it's not right for a girl to be seen like that."

"Ay, Mamá, I don't care if I'm seen like that." Mariana was used to the way her mother spoke of how Ricardo had courted her. When he came to her house, he stayed outside and spoke to her through a window because her father would not allow any men in his home. She did not want that fate for herself. "Los Zamora are my friends and we don't do anything wrong. I just want to have a good time. Just because you . . ."

"Mariana!" Sofía did not like to raise her voice at her daughter, but lately she was doing it quite a bit. It was difficult to argue with her, and it tired Sofía. Her strength was no longer enough for the weekly screaming match. "You don't speak to me like that. Soy tu madre and I say you are not going out tonight."

Mariana slammed the hairbrush down on top of the dresser. "And I say I am! I don't want to be stuck sewing pillowcases all night. You just want me here so the entire pueblo doesn't talk about us the way they do. But they're right, Mamá, my father's not coming back! ¡Nos abandonó! And he's not going to come back if I stay home. He's not going to come back if I go out. He's not going to come back if *you* go out. He's never coming back!"

"¡Basta, Mariana! No vas a hablar mal de tu papá. He's working and he misses us. The money he sends us is what bought that dress you're wearing. Ten respeto."

Mariana turned her back on her mother and stared at her reflection. "Respeto. What respeto did he have when he left us? He probably has a brand new house over there while we have to live here and you're worried about respeto and what the neighbors will say."

Sofía clenched her fists and teeth to keep from slapping her daughter. Ricardo had never spanked Mariana and had told Sofía not to do it, either. Hitting was for animals, he'd said, and no child of his was going to be treated that way. "Your father is going to come back one of these days, and when he does, he's going to be very disappointed in you, Mariana. He used to be so proud of you. He'd take you all around the plaza and brag that his daughter was more beautiful than la Reina de la Feria that year. Now look what you've become."

"I haven't become anything that he isn't. Why can he leave and not care about what happens to us, but I can't have fun for awhile? I go to school, Mamá. You can't expect more than that. The weekends are my time. I'm going out with Marisol and her brothers. I'm not going to stay locked up behind four walls. Not tonight, not ever, just like my father."

Sofía felt defeated. She had tried dozens of times to make her daughter see that her father had not abandoned them. She wanted Mariana to make him proud. But nothing ever worked. She knew if she kept arguing with her daughter, she'd only end up in tears. She resigned herself with a last attempt. "Don't you dare set foot outside of this house. I'm warning you."

She dared to hope that Mariana would not defy her this time. Maybe Father Jacinto was right. She just had to remain strong and not give in. It was probably a battle of wills. That child was not going to win this one.

But Mariana opened the door and stepped out. "I already told Marisol that I was going and I'm not going to let her down. You are not going to stop me. It is my life!"

"Mariana! Get back in here. I don't want to have to drag you in from the street." Before Sofía could reach her, the young girl closed the door. Sofía pounded on it with both fists. She would never really put her daughter through the shame of being dragged in from the street. "Dios will punish you for this! ¡Hija, entiende! The earth will swallow you. God will punish you, Mariana. Come back."

She rested her forehead against the wooden door, letting the sobs and tears escape. She was losing her daughter and she didn't know how to hold on anymore. It had to be because of Marisol and her brothers. Those kids never did learn to respect their parents. That Marisol must have some type of brujería.

"Mamá!" Mariana's screams broke through Sofía's thoughts. Her voice sounded angry still. "Get me out of here!"

Sofía walked outside and was met by the evening's dark sky and warm breezes. Mariana was not in the yard. Sofía walked down the porch steps, heading for the road, but stopped halfway there and waited. The hardened soil was still warm under her toes. Again, she heard Mariana yell. "Get over here and get me out." Sofiá's eyes automatically glanced to her right. A few meters ahead of her, she finally saw Mariana.

In the soft white light of the night's moon, Sofía saw her daughter struggling to lift herself from a hole in the dry earth. A relieved sigh escaped her chest. "Ay, Mariana, are you all right? You scared me. ¿Qué pasó? I'm sure your dress is ruined now. But I told you that's what happens when you don't listen to me."

"Ya, enough, stop talking and get me out. Now I'm going to have to change and I'm going to be late." Mariana grabbed her mother's hands and tried to lift herself up.

"Ay, mija, you're heavy." Sofía pulled, but her daughter would not budge. "When I find out what chamacos were out digging in our yard . . . Ay, mija, help me out here. I can't do it by myself. You're too big for me."

"I'm trying!" Mariana twisted herself left and right as she pulled on her mother's hands, but she could not lift herself out. "No, this isn't working. We're going to have to dig. The dirt must have fallen in with me. Hurry up! It's cold in this thing and there's probably all sorts of spiders and alacranes in here."

Mariana had fallen in as far as her chest and Sofía wondered how she had managed to miss such a hole when she came home herself. She got down on her knees and scratched at the dirt. Mariana was right. The soil was cold around her body, but warm under Sofía's knees. Something was happening to her daughter, but Sofía became too scared to question it. She continued to claw at the ground, realizing it was as if a spell had been cast upon the dry earth. As she dug up fistfuls of soil, more of it appeared to take its place. Mariana dug as well, but even that did not help. The earth had a tight grip on the lower half of Mariana's body.

"What's happening, Mamá?" Mariana's anger was mounting. "Why can't I get out?"

"No sé, mija." Sofía's voice trembled. "Maybe you're moving and it makes the soil fall back in." She began to work faster, but made no progress.

When she finally ran out of strength and breath, she looked up at her daughter. Mariana was crying. "No, mija." Sofía put a hand to her daughter's face smudging her chin with dirt. "We're going to get you out. Just let me rest a little bit."

But Mariana's tears were not of sadness. "No, Mamá, I know what's happening. Tú lo dijiste when I closed the door. I heard you! Dijiste que la tierra me iba a tragar. Mamá, it really happened. I'm going to die here!" She grabbed handfuls of dirt from around herself and threw them about angrily. "I'm going to die here!"

Sofía hugged her daughter and cried herself. "No, mija, I didn't mean that. I was angry at you, sí, pero no era en serio. Tenía mucho coraje, pero Dios no puede hacer esto. It was just a saying, mija. Those things don't really happen. I'm going to get you out, you'll see." Sofía wanted to believe her own words, but she had been digging for a long while and, although there were mounds of dirt strewn about, she had not managed to make a dent in the soil around her daughter.

Mariana pushed her mother away. "Stop this, already. ¿No entiendes? You did this to me! You had to have the last word and you did this to me! Now I'm going to die here and it's all your fault!" She laughed out loud as she clawed at the dirt under her chest. "It's happening, Mamá. You made it happen. You killed your own daughter! What will the town say about that?"

"No, mija. I'm going to get you out." Sofía resumed her digging. Mounds of dirt grew higher around them while the earth that held Mariana's torso remained as high as when it opened up to swallow her. Sofía's efforts continued until the sound of footsteps on the road jolted her out of her obsession.

Tired of waiting for Mariana, Marisol had walked over to her friend's house. The sight of the two women in the cold dirt confused and scared her at the same time. She stopped a few feet away from them and tried to figure out what was going on. "¿Qué tiene Mariana?" She could hardly see behind Sofía who was on her hands and knees, clawing at the ground.

At having to explain her daughter's predicament and her own failed efforts, Sofía burst into tears again. "No sé. We had a fight. I told her not to go out. Y se abrió la tierra. I didn't mean it. I was just so mad at her. I can't get her out." She reached for another fistful of dirt and threw it at the road. "I can't get her out!"

Marisol knelt beside Mariana. "¿Qué te pasó?" Mariana folded her arms and motioned over to her mother with a brisk movement of her shoulder, "Me mató mi mamá." It did not sound like a joke to Marisol, but Mariana's tone told her not to ask any questions. She turned her attention to the soil and helped Sofía dig. She did not understand why Mariana wasn't helping as well, but she was afraid to look up at her.

Marisol noticed that not much was happening as she and Sofía dug, but assumed that the soil was just too hard. After a couple of minutes, however, Marisol looked at Sofía. "¿Por qué no pasa nada?"

Sofía did not stop to look at her, "No sé. Keep going. Tú también tienes la culpa. If you didn't keep dragging my daughter with you and those buenos pa' nada brothers of yours—"

"Mamá!" Mariana shook Sofía's shoulder. "¡No le digas eso! None of this is her fault. It happened after you yelled at me, remember?"

Sofía did not answer. Instead, she motioned to Marisol to keep digging.

But Marisol was too scared that Sofía might be right. She got up and dusted the soil off her legs. She turned toward the road and said the only thing that came to mind, "I'll go get Father Jacinto." She ran down the road toward the church.

❧┄━┄❧

When the sun rose the next morning, a crowd of people was gathered together in Sofía's front yard. They repeated the words "ruega por ella" over and over as Father Jacinto read down a list of saints. Mariana looked up at all of them and mumbled that they could at least wait until she was dead before they prayed for her. After hearing Sofía's story and watching for himself the failed efforts of several who tried to dig her out with hands, sticks, buckets, and shovels, the elderly priest had deemed the previous night's supernatural occurrences a punishment from God. Therefore, the only thing that could be done was to pray that God would see fit to release Mariana from her prison. Even if Mariana complained about the entire thing and seemed to delight in her statement that her own mother had killed her, Father Jacinto was convinced that he could perform a miracle.

He had sent Marisol to gather more people in order to have a stronger voice and message to send to the heavens. He also wanted a stronger message to send to the pueblo itself. Whether out of faith or chisme, the entire town turned out. The women gathered around the priest and followed the prayers. The men formed a group nearer to the road and came up with their own reasons for Mariana's situation. The children preferred to sit around Mariana to interrogate her about the hole. Mariana repeatedly instructed them to go away.

A couple of the Zamora brothers, not wanting Mariana to suffer in the blazing sun for as long as it took God to let her out, had taken an armful of firewood along with one of Sofía's embroidered tablecloths and built a shelter over Mariana's head. Marisol brought food and drink out for her friend and helped keep the curious children far enough away from Mariana. Yet the ground around Mariana remained cold. Several people lay candles, crucifixes, rosaries, and santos around Mariana to ward off any more evil. But even a full town's prayers, ideas, questions, and artwork were not enough to convince God.

Sofía knelt near her daughter, alternating between prayers, pleas for forgiveness, striking deals with God, and loud sobs. She wanted God to punish her instead. Mariana agreed. "I shouldn't be the one in here. I have a full life to live. See what you did to me? What would mi querido papi say about this? I bet he wouldn't care. He hasn't cared about anything that's happened to me for the last three years."

Sofía did not have the strength to argue with her daughter. "Ya, hija, I know you're right. Pero, we have to do something. The only thing we have left is to pray for a miracle. God will listen to us. Look at everyone who came out to help us. It's going to happen. No te preocupes."

"To help us?" Mariana shook her mother's shoulder. "Nobody's here to help us. Look at them. They're loving this. I'm the most exciting thing that ever happened in La Victoria. They don't want to help me. Quieren el chisme."

"Mariana, por favor. We're all trying to ask God for you, but you have to help us. Mija, try to have faith."

"Faith for what? I'm not getting out of here and everybody knows it. I just want to know how long I'm going to have to sit here and listen to all of you. Why doesn't everybody just leave me alone?"

Down the road, a large pick-up truck made its way to Sofía's house. It raised a cloud of dust behind it as it wound around the last curve and stopped near the group of men. The back of the truck was full of gente of all ages who stared around at the crowd as the driver leaned out the window and tilted his sombrero back. "¿Es aquí donde se tragó la tierra a una muchacha?" Word of the swallowing had gotten out and was reaching other pueblos and ranchos.

"Todavía no se la traga," one of the men answered, "Allá está." He pointed towards Mariana's colorful shelter.

The driver turned off the engine and motioned for everyone to get out. "Venimos de San Felipe. We heard the news out there and figured we should come see for ourselves. El chisme está llegando por toda la región. People are saying that this is a good way to teach the chamacos to obey. A ver si así se portan bien los canijos. ¿A poco si se la está tragando la tierra? You men sure it's not just a hole?"

The men looked around at each other until the one who had spoken up earlier finally did so again. "Pos, ya le escarbamos. We used everything we could. We even dug farther away to make a tunnel to her. You're not going to believe me, pero we never did find her legs under there. I say the devil has a hand in this and it's better just to stay away from it." The rest of the men nodded their agreement and soon began talking about the lack of rain and the damage to their crops.

A parade of more trucks followed the first one. Some of the passengers did not bother to get out, but stared at Mariana through their windows before leaving again. Others ventured to ask, "Did that really happen because she disobeyed her mother?" The men assured them all that it did. They were enjoying the attention they were receiving. After a while, the story had been embellished by multiple accounts. Mariana was accused of everything from leaving without permission to attacking her mother with a piece of firewood. "Esa muchacha trae el demonio metido," was the general consensus among the travelers.

Father Jacinto saw an opportunity to increase faith and church attendance by turning Mariana's fate into an example for all who would listen. When full classrooms of schoolchildren arrived, he motioned for them to step closer. He gathered them around him the way he did when he taught his catechism classes on Saturdays. After blessing them all, he told them to pay attention to what he was going to say. "This story is going to affect all of you because each one of you has parents you must obey."

He led his flock closer to Mariana and began his lecture in a voice much like that of a ringmaster announcing the feats of the trapeze artists. "This poor girl was punished for not doing as her mother said. Mariana wanted to go to a dance. Her mother, this poor disconsolate woman, said no. But Mariana decided to go anyway, and she did. She shut the door in her mother's face." The children moved away from Father Jacinto to form a semicircle around Mariana. They stared wide-eyed back and forth from her to Father Jacinto and did not dare utter a word while he spoke.

"Poor Sofía," the old Padre continued, "Her grief consumed her and she was sick with worry over her daughter's sinful habits. She came to me many times for advice on how to lead her back to the right path. Together we tried and tried to tell Mariana that the Lord says children must obey their parents." He looked from child to child as Mariana rolled her eyes at the entire scene. She had not spoken to the priest since the one and only time two and a half years ago that he came to her house to try to straighten her out. She told him then that she was not interested in anything he had to say and had sent him on his way with his Bible and advice intact. Father Jacinto had never returned and was now blatantly lying to these chamacos. "Go to hell," she whispered to herself.

Father Jacinto was on a mission. "Mariana never listened to either one of us. It seemed she was only interested in having fun. Poor Sofía shed lágrimas de sangre until she could withstand it no longer." Father Jacinto walked over to Sofía and put his hands on her shoulders. "We must understand that this woman tried everything to help her daughter see her evil ways." Sofía looked at the ground, embarrassed by the attention the priest was bringing to her. "Ya, Padre, I think this is too much."

Father Jacinto ignored her comment and continued his lecture for the children. "We all know that a mother's curse is sacrosanct. Everything about your own mother is to be respected. This poor woman in her desperation cursed her only daughter. She told her the earth would swallow her. It did. Hijos míos, do not suffer the same fate as this poor child. Jesus Christ, our Lord, set an example for us to follow, and God, our Father, set it in stone so that we might never forget it; honor thy father and thy mother."

With that, he turned to Mariana and solemnly asked, "My child, why did the earth open up under you? What sin did you commit that God is punishing you like this?" While his words were soft-spoken, he shot Mariana a look that told her she had better play into his game plan.

Mariana looked at the soil around her chest, at her mother, at Father Jacinto, and finally at the children around her homemade altar. "I disobeyed my mother," she muttered through her teeth. A sarcastic smile crossed her lips as a gasp of shock came from the children. Father Jacinto's wrinkled face let out a heavy sigh. Mariana played the part of the guilty disobedient daughter with a twinkle in her eyes. "I yelled at her and left without her permission. Now, what my mother told me came true. You guys shouldn't disobey your mother, but if you do, make sure you don't give her a chance to—"

"Hijos míos," Father Jacinto interrupted Mariana, "this child has much soul-searching to do. We should leave her alone." After warning the children that they, too, could be swallowed up by the earth if they were disobedient sons and daughters, he made them all promise to attend mass every Sunday and always do as they were told. The children nodded their heads and mumbled their promises to the priest. When he was convinced the children were scared into religion and proper behavior, Father Jacinto sent them home in the name of the Father, the Son, and the Holy Spirit.

By nightfall, Mariana's patience and enjoyment of the game had faded. She had put up with the obedience lecture all day and seen too many curious faces come close to her. "Stop praying," she told the last remaining señoras. Most of the locals were now inside the house enjoying her mother's coffee and spiking it with "un piquetito." "I'm not going to get out." She motioned for her mother and Father Jacinto to come closer. "Don't pray for that. Pray that I die soon. Pray that the earth will do its job and finish me up. I don't want to be a circus freak again tomorrow when more people show up to stare at me."

Sofía rushed to her daughter's side and fell to her knees. "Hija, no digas eso. We'll get you out. Have faith." She took her daughter's face in her hands and was surprised at what she saw. Mariana's eyes were calm and her lips almost curved into a smile. "Mamá, it is not going to happen. I am not going to get out of here. I wish everyone would stop acting like they're waiting for a miracle that's never going to come. Nobody really wants me to get out. I'm la mala hija, remember? I'm the black sheep, la hija pródiga. I've had enough of this show. Prayers aren't getting me out. Ya me maldijiste una vez and it worked. Curse me again and finish the job. Go ahead, Mami, wish me dead."

The pain Sofía felt in her chest almost knocked her over. "¡Nunca! Hija, I can't do that. Primero me muero yo. You're going to get out, I promise. Just try to have faith in God, please."

Mariana looked at her mother for a while and decided on a new strategy. Sofía wanted her sweet, innocent daughter back. Very well, then. She softened her tone as she spoke again. "Mamita, perdóname. I did not mean to be a bad daughter. I wanted to be good, but I was so angry at mi papá for leaving us behind. I know I was wrong. You've prayed all day, Mami. Now, I want you to understand that this is what God wants."

Sofía stared back at her daughter. She could not believe what she was hearing. "I'll be fine now, Mami. Tell Father Jacinto to ask God for me. You are going to have to be strong and wait until mi papi comes back so you won't be alone. It won't be long, Mami. I have to go. It's what God wants. But you need to help me, Amá. You need to finish the curse. Go get Father Jacinto. Please." The peace in Mariana's voice sent a chill down Sofía's spine, but she did as her daughter asked.

As her mother walked away, Mariana searched out Marisol's eyes. She smiled at her and saw in Marisol's face that she understood what was happening. Marisol only shook her head. Mariana giggled softly.

When Father Jacinto stood next to them, Sofía lowered her head. "Padre, please forgive me for what I'm about to do." Father Jacinto placed his hand on Sofía's head. "In the name of God our Father, I forgive you, hija."

Sofía knelt to kiss her daughter, but she could not bear to look at her as she spoke. She straightened herself and turned her back. "Que sea lo que Dios quiera. I leave it up to Him. Que te trague la tierra, hija mía. Ya te veré en la Santa Gloria."

Father Jacinto looked toward the heavens and uttered a plea. "Please, Father, end this child's torment. Forgive her trespasses and welcome her into a better life."

The earth around Mariana loosened and pulled her down. With a final blessing from Father Jacinto's right hand, the rest of Mariana's body sank slowly into the earth's womb. The dirt seemed to breathe and expand, making room for her. When her shoulders disappeared, Mariana looked up at her mother. "Gracias, Mamá," she said with a sharp edge in her voice that only Marisol fully understood. Mariana smiled as she lowered her head into the earth.

Sofía, her eyes closed, heard murmurs coming from the group of señoras who had gathered closer. "Mira nada más." "Como si la estuviera esperando el suelo." "Seguro que se va a ir hasta abajo." Sofía brought her hands to her ears and bit her lip to keep from yelling at the chismosas who were so sure her daughter would keep falling straight into hell. She bent her head and loudly whispered an Ave María.

When Sofía looked back, the soil under the shelter was spotless. The crosses, candles and saints formed a circle around the spot where her daughter had spent her last day. The world went black as she felt her body fall heavily onto the ground.

A white stone cross was placed at the spot of Mariana's second birth. The people who stop by to pray there say that no matter how hot the day is, the soil around the cross is freezing cold. They say it is because Mariana never really was sorry and her soul just sits there waiting for someone to pray enough to send her to heaven.

ALTAR

Kathleen Alcalá

AT DAWN THEY THREW THE SAND PAINTING IN THE RIVER.

It had represented the need to let go of emotional attachments, and as Shell had sat in the darkened room where the sand painting was being painstakingly constructed, ignoring the discomfort of the metal chair, he had concentrated on just that, taking his attachment to each of the people in his past, holding it up like a fluttering prayer flag in the wind—and letting go. But the motif in the mandala that stayed with him, following him around as he sorted through the mail and delivered it each day, was the skull and bones, skull and bones, skull and bones. An unmistakable symbol in any culture.

The Tibetan priests had been invited to visit this almost-at-the-cutting-edge town in southern Colorado, so they stayed for a few days to share their Zen stuff or their karma or whatever it was that they shared.

At the urging of a coworker at the post office, Shell had agreed to let two of the young priests stay with him. They did not speak English, but it didn't seem to matter. He just showed them the kitchen—flicking the stove on and off, showed them the bathroom, flushing the toilet once—and they threw down bedrolls in his tiny living room each night. Since they never went into the bedroom, Shell didn't need to explain the fur mantle in the closet. He had moved his makeup out of the bathroom. Once he met them, Shell doubted that they would have cared. Something about these guys was so beyond physicality that, if Shell had had the words to explain, he felt they would have understood immediately.

This was unlike his own family, the people whose faces appeared on the imaginary prayer flags Shell was releasing one by one into the wind. Whose history with him slipped into the river with the elaborate sand painting that the priests spent three days creating before its destruction. To desire nothing was to achieve nirvana. But after twenty-eight years, Shell had not, could not shake the desire to be something other than what he was.

Abbott, Abbey, Acuña. Bell, Beller, Blount, Butler. Conrad, Contreras (lots of Contrerases), Cain, Mark of.

That's how he had always felt. Cain had been altered, Shell was convinced, to set him apart for the remainder of his life, to cause others to avoid him while staring and pointing. He had been denied his place among the birds of the air and the beasts of the field, forced to lead the lonely existence of the outcast.

All his life Shell had borne this difference, this mark, and had felt sure that it too was apparent to everyone. It had driven him to this place, this state and this town, to seek out the doctor whose name he had carried on a smudged paper torn from a pharmaceutical company pad.

"It's not easy," the referring physician had said. "It's a long road to follow."

But I'm already on it, Shell wanted to say. I've been on it since I was born.

Shell had to be at work at five, and he liked rising early. A little sustenance, a big stretch, and he was off for the post office. He couldn't tell if the enhancements were visible to others yet, but he at least imagined that he could tell the difference in the early morning light, before the sun burst over the mountain range and flooded the valley in flat light.

Each morning when he arose, the young monks were already up. He did not know when they slept, but he envied them their stamina. As much as he worked out now, Shell did not have the strength or agility to perform the feats that really appealed to him, that would be necessary to survive in his new life. His diet had been the hardest thing to hide while the monks were visiting, but he solved that by eating out most of the time they were there. If they looked in the freezer, they kept it to themselves.

The only decoration in Shell's spare apartment was a print of the *Feast of Tlacaxipehualiztli* from the *Book of the Life of the Ancient Mexicans*. It depicted two warriors, one tied to a large, round stone, the other dressed in the skin of a jaguar. The Tibetan monks had admired it at length on the first day, gesturing at it and then at Shell, as though they saw the resemblance. Shell had felt the blood rise to his face, but since he couldn't speak to them, he just smiled and pretended that they were merely complementing him on his good taste.

God only knows what it means in their iconography, thought Shell. But to him it meant rebirth through blood, reincarnation of the flesh into flesh, a higher self, a truer self, in this life rather than the next. Shell thought he understood blood sacrifice perfectly. And yet these mild-mannered rice-eaters smiled and nodded and sat down with his print as though it were an old, familiar friend. Perhaps it was, he thought.

Once Shell had agreed to let the monks stay with him, it was suggested that he attend the local Sangha in order to familiarize himself with their practices. The Sangha turned out to be a motley collection of aging hippies, former Catholic nuns, and the sort of youth who would have been drawn to the Baha'i a generation earlier. Shell had nothing in common with them, but he appreciated the nonjudgmental aura that rose from their collective body. Shell had been the subject of hard stares too often recently to shrug them off, drawing the attention of flinty-eyed ranchers in town for a few supplies.

Drew, Dorado, Darwin. Shell often wondered—as his fingers flipped rapidly through the letters, stuffing them into the right cubbies—if any of these people were related to their famous namesakes. They might be, he thought, and imagined presenting himself to Joseph

Darwin and saying, "Well?" Shell could imagine the look on the old man's face (they had never met, but Darwin received frequent mailings from the AARP) as he took in the full extent of Shell's self-propelled evolution. A lonely path indeed.

The chanting, much to Shell's surprise, soothed his soul. There was no other way to describe it. As he sat on his haunches on the floor of the Masonic Temple where the Sangha met, the rising and falling of their untrained voices resolved itself into a song like that of the cicadas in late summer. While Shell would never master the deep, dual tones of the throat-singing he would later hear from the monks, it allowed him to explore the full extent of his vocal register.

When he moved to this town surrounded by mountains, its history spelled out in bricks and the blood of mine workers, Shell had ceased communicating with his parents. The late-born child of immigrants, it hadn't been too hard. When it became clear that Shell was not interested in marrying and producing grandchildren, his parents turned most of their attention to his older brothers and sisters, the "breeders," as he thought of them. He still called one of his brothers now and then, but Shell doubted that he would have recognized him had they passed on the street.

The job was over by 3 P.M., which gave Shell a chance to nap in the afternoon. This seemed so natural to him, that he wondered why he hadn't done it all his life. At night, well, at night the world was alive.

The famous doctor had seen it all. Aging drag queens, same-sex couples in love, twin brothers who both suffered from sexual dissonance. But after spending forty-five minutes with Shell and going over his medical records again and again, the doctor had shaken his head and stood up behind his desk.

"I'm sorry," he said. "But I'll really have to think about this first. And do some research."

"You're my last hope," said Shell, as a muffling darkness seemed to creep in around him. "I've even begun to live as one, as much as possible."

The doctor refused to make eye contact. "I'll have to get back to you," he said, "after I make a few calls."

Shell spent the next two weeks in a gray fog, trying to keep his funk from affecting his productivity at work. He needed to earn as much money as possible while he could. One of the women on his route began leaving cookies hung on the mailbox decorated to resemble happy faces. He dumped them at the end of the day in the large receptacle provided for the inevitable human debris that came with the job.

He thought perhaps he could manage it without the operations, but he didn't know how long he would survive. Shell raised his grief-filled voice in chant and sat endlessly in meditation, feeling his feet, then his ankles, calves, and knees go numb. If I cannot tolerate this, he thought, then I can tolerate nothing. I am nothing.

He humbled himself. He learned. And to his surprise, the doctor called back.

"Well," he said, clearing his throat, "I can't find any reason for you not to pursue this." The doctor paused. "So come in next week and we will at least make a plan."

The doctor had obtained information on similar cases in Germany. Germany! He had heard rumors in the clubs, of course. The places he had gone in Los Angeles and New York and Chicago, seeking others like himself. He had enjoyed some of it, the sheer exhibitionism of some people. But most of the time, Shell had been repulsed by the deviations he had encountered, desires that left him all the more inclined to go in another direction.

"We can follow these cases," the doctor continued, "and see what works and what doesn't. As they perform surgeries, the attending physicians can send me photos and instructions."

The doctor outlined a regimen for Shell, a combination of diet and exercise. He would have to take supplements if he were going to adhere to a high protein diet. His digestive tract would be unable to extract all of the necessary vitamins and minerals from a diet of raw meat. Shell purchased the freshest beef and chicken he could find, musing on the frank carnality of our existence as he divided it into smaller portions.

"You realize," said the surgeon, "that I can only take you so far before you run into some very practical questions."

Shell thought he was going to be referred to a psychiatrist, another rocky road he had already traveled.

"I mean basics. Once you have undergone even the simpler surgeries, like having your digits shortened and your palms augmented, how

will you make a living? You can't sort mail. How will you support yourself? Once we have shortened your thighs and tibias, where will you
live? You will be unable to walk upright for any length of time. I can't
allow you to endanger yourself or others in this process."

Shell felt his face close down.

"But you've been told all this, haven't you?"

Shell nodded.

"And you don't care."

"No," said Shell softly.

"Well, I'm only a surgeon."

But this time Shell detected something else in the doctor's voice,
the sound of a man who enjoys a challenge.

It took about an hour from the initial prayers over the sand mandala that morning to the careful transportation of it down the hill, past
the public park, to the modest concrete bridge that crossed the river.
The local police had closed it to vehicles that Sunday morning, forcing
churchgoers down to the next bridge to drive into town.

Four priests held the mandala aloft in the morning light, including
one of the young monks who had stayed with Shell. His skin glistened
with good health, his bare arms were defined by muscles that easily lifted the round tabletop bearing the fragile sand painting high overhead.
His robes, the same color as marigolds, rustled slightly as he tilted his
head back in seeming exultation. The inexorable sun topped the mountains and bathed him in golden light.

To let go. To release earthly attachments and be free. They tipped
the table and a rainbow stream spilled over the bridge railing into the
muddy waters below.

And Shell let go too of the one impulse, the last earthly desire that
had held him prisoner all these lonely years. He let go of the image of
the one person to whom he had confessed his great need in hopes that
he would understand and accompany him on this journey. Shell had
never forgotten the look of confusion and fear, the deep feeling of
shame that had swept over him. In Shell's mind, the shining eyes and
dark hair floated off into the air, joining the other images he had
released over the last days and weeks. Shell felt weightless, suspended
between worlds.

In three great bounds he reached the center of the bridge and seized the young monk by the shoulders. Shell pinned him to the road and ripped his throat out with his teeth, the copper taste of blood running down his own throat.

Shell was filled with an indescribable warmth even as he realized he had thrown it all away. He was vaguely aware of people screaming, of being pulled back from his prey.

To desire nothing. To feel nothing. To be nothing.

The expression on the young monk's face as the life force left him was, Shell was certain, a look of recognition.

TEAR OUT MY HEART

Torie Olson

AT 8 A.M., AURORA OPENS THE CAFE AT THE CASA LUNA. SHE UNLOCKS the heavy wooden door that bears a spectacular carving of San Miguel the devil slayer. Right away, she is busy whisking coffee to customers who sit under the white umbrellas in her courtyard. She brings them mango jam, a basket of bolillos, and a small bowl of salsa verde. In between tasks, she takes quick drags of a cigarette and greets the Chichimeca in the blue rebozo.

This is the Indian who sleeps on a striped serape just outside Aurora's door. During the day, she sells her handmade cloth dolls, although sometimes she just holds out her palm. Aurora does not give her pesos. Instead, she serves the Chichimeca her favorite dishes—garlic steak, stuffed pumpkin flowers, and flan de caramelo. Aurora would feed the world if she could. Certainly, she would feed the women of the world. And their children. No hungry children. No dead ones, either.

Miguel Hernández is of the same mind. Despite his Spanish blood and monied class, he is an outspoken patron of the people. There has been another slaughter of the indígenas—always the mothers and children—so Miguel will leave this morning in support of the revolutionaries. He will go to the capital to put red bandanas on the statues at the Plaza de la Independencia, to place a small coffin there for each murdered one, and to make speeches that end in "¡Ya Basta!" Enough Already!

But before leaving, Miguel climbs a ladder and scrawls a poem on the cafe wall. It is a verse to La Luz del Norte, his northern light, which is what he calls his Aurora.

Sometimes she calls him San Miguel because he wants so much to rid the world of devils, and because, after all these years, she still thinks of him as her own archangel.

The Casa Luna has been in Miguel's family for over 300 years, and it has been Aurora's refuge since New Year's Day in 1959.

The night before, she had fled across the border into Mexico—not because of her country's politics or poverty—but to outrun a bad man, her husband. Because of one mistake, she'd been thrown off her ranch, committed to an asylum, and hunted across the Southwest. This bad man had burned her things, destroyed her gardens, and stolen her child.

Aurora knows how to recognize a bad man. There is one staying at Casa Luna right now. He is also a wealthy Americano. He is also a husband. Also, his wife is very young.

Aurora was twenty-four when she fought her way through the pucker brush to the cantina on the other side. There she managed to hitchhike a ride south. She was let out in a thorny no-man's land, but she walked on through the night in her thin white dress. Cold and exhausted, she'd finally curled up behind a giant maguey plant.

A Huichole had been walking in the same direction. He was on his annual pilgrimage in the stony north where the sacred peyote grows. He'd spotted her by the cactus, glowing like the moon in her white clothes, and thought she was a goddess. All night, under the burning stars, he'd watched over her, and at times he heard her weeping.

The bad man's young wife has red eyes from crying. The man says it is just from the dust. But Aurora does not believe him for one moment.

She had trusted the Huichole instinctively. He'd appeared at first light, offering his pitahayas, the red fruits of the prickly pear, and pouring her a drink of pulque. He'd tried to speak to her in Nahuatl, the language of the marketplace, but she hadn't understood, so he'd used the little Spanish he knew from selling his beaded animal carvings to the tourists.

The bad man speaks no Spanish, but the girl had three years of it in high school. Aurora thinks she should be back there now, getting ready to be a prom queen. She's too young to be the wife of this Robert Redford look-alike and too fair to be here in the Mexican sun. Already, Aurora thinks, she is wilting.

Aurora had followed the Huichole across the altiplano to this town of light and shadow. He also wore white clothing, although his cuffs and sleeves were embroidered with bands of birds. On top of this, he wore a red cape and a straw hat stuck with eagle feathers. He carried votive sticks that he left for his gods at intervals along the way.

He brought Aurora to the town square or jardín, as it is called here, and despite the hubbub of the chalupa sellers, child beggars, and boat-tailed grackles in the laurel trees, she fell asleep. When she awoke, Miguel Hernández was sitting on the same park bench.

"Nuevo Año," he murmured, offering her a cigarette. Then he gestured to the Huichole who was keeping watch from across the square. "The Indian calls you La Llorona. Do you know who that is?"

Aurora ran her hands through her long, uncombed hair and shook her head.

"She is the Weeping Woman," Miguel replied, "The Aztec goddess who roams the countryside. She is always clad in white, and crying for her lost child."

". . . and I am wearing white," she said, trying to straighten her wrinkled dress.

"Seeing La Llorona is a bad omen," Miguel added. "It makes the Indians afraid for their own children."

"Please explain to him that I am just an American."

"So why does an American arrive in the early light?" Miguel asked. "And why does she come on foot behind the medicine man from Jalisco?"

"It's a long story."

"Well, you see," Miguel said, "I am a poet, so I'm always looking for a story. I am also very hungry, so why don't you join me for breakfast at my father's house? Then you can tell me about your adventures."

"I am Aurora Peckham Hood," is how she began on the day the Huichole and the Zapatista poet offered her their protection for life. "I am in your country illegally, but you must understand that I have come here from hell."

The well-connected Hernández family had used its influence to get Aurora a permanent visa and set her up in business. The fiery-eyed Miguel got her a divorce and tried to marry her, but although he did manage to get her out of that white dress that spooked the Indian so, she has refused his ring for over two decades.

Miguel also worked through official and unofficial channels to find Aurora's daughter, but after several months of inquiry, he found a death certificate instead.

Aurora still mourns this child. Every year on the Day of the Dead, she buys a candy skull for Molly and places it on the flowered altar.

Miguel provided a second daughter, however—not one of their intimacy because Aurora could not bear to have another that way—but a child from a family of curanderas, some say witches. Her name is Guadalupe, and she has the mysterious eyes of her namesake, the dark-skinned Virgin and the patroness of the Americas. She is the real daughter of the woman who lives on the pavement just outside the door.

Lupe is nineteen now and the second in command at Casa Luna. She is the one who registered the bad man and the girl, his wife. Wearing a white linen suit, the man had flashed his pesos around and asked for the best room in the house. He'd chosen the red room with its spiky iron headboard and the wall of folk art masks once used in the sacred animal dances.

The red room is the one with the view. It looks out over the place where the Aztecs once made their bloody offerings—the hearts of young girls, torn out of their living bodies with obsidian blades. But the gods are no longer fed there. The old spot has been covered up with a pink church, and now it is the young girls, dressed in carnation crowns and hoop skirts for their first communion, who taste the blood and the body of Christ. Sometimes these celebrations end up at the Casa Luna because Aurora's cafe is known for the best breakfast in town.

On her first morning, the girl breakfasts alone at the table under the orange tree. She orders a pot of hot chocolate. Nothing else.

"And your husband," Aurora asks, as she pours the rich froth into a blue-flowered cup, "is he sleeping off too many Margaritas?"

"Maybe, if you're talking about women," the girl says, although Aurora cannot tell if she is serious or not.

When the man comes down, there are dark shadows under his eyes, and he is wearing the same linen suit. He lights a cigarrito and does not look at his wife. "Coffee Americano," he tells Aurora.

The girl knocks over the basket of bolillos by accident. When Aurora bends down to pick the rolls off the stones, she notices the bright purple plum on the back of the girl's calf.

The man picks up a newspaper and hides behind the screen of print. Lupe brings new rolls, and the girl splits one, sweetens it with jam, and hands it behind the screen. She does this until the straw basket is empty. Aurora sees that she has eaten nothing, and thinks, this man is breaking her heart.

Aurora's broken heart was mended by Miguel, a man with money and looks and also compassion. For over two decades, she has been his lover and muse. In verse, he has described her eyes, green like the saguaro cactus; her rosy skin, blushing like mangoes; her hair, the color of a dark red mole. And what woman would argue with a man who claims she only looks two-thirds her age?

Today is Aurora's fifty-second birthday, and Miguel has given her the opals in her ears and the seven silver bracelets around her wrists. She is also wearing the white peasant shirt he has brought her from the bottom of his country. There are three other packages on the counter, but they have come for the man who is staying in the red room.

Aurora takes these to his table now. After he has opened them, he makes a call to America, and Aurora hears him shouting into the phone.

In the afternoon, the Huichole, who continues after all these years to look after her, comes with a warning. Aurora puts a plate of chicken flautas and guacamole before him and he tells her there will be a frost. Although there haven't been more than two or three this century, Aurora knows the Indian will be proven right. She asks Lupe's uncle,

Don Antonio, to pick up the drop cloths from the rooms he is painting to drape over her vines and trees.

Aurora is famous for her gardens, especially the bougainvilleas, jacarandas, four-o'clocks, and gloriosa lilies that tumble down the old palacio walls. When tourists ask her secret, she nods to the terra-cotta sculpture under the angel trumpet tree. And with a twinkle in her green eyes, she explains, "He is Xochipili, the Aztec prince of flowers and the enchanter of my garden." She also cooks for her plants, following recipes for biodynamic teas and barrel composts, which she applies during the correct phase of the moon.

When the moon rises that night, it is almost full, and there is a freak ring around it.

In the morning, Aurora unveils her vines, and they are their usual floriferous selves. Everyone else's have dropped their blossoms, and their leaves have turned a sickly yellow.

When the girl comes down, she also looks sickly. Aurora seats her by the orange tree again, and notices that her pale skin has the same greenish tinge that white flowers do. Again, the man comes later and ignores his wife at breakfast. As far as Aurora can tell, these two do not look like honeymooners at all.

The Huichole comes again, and Aurora brings him a piece of lime pie and a papaya shake. The man pushes back his chair with a screech and asks to be introduced to the Indian. He wants to talk about peyote. Aurora translates.

"A small amount takes away hunger, thirst, and tiredness," the Huichole says. "If you take more, it is possible to gain wisdom."

When the man has gone away, the Huichole says, "Something is not right at the Casa Luna." And before he leaves, he plants four god's eyes in a line between the red room and the big wooden door.

There is a lot of noise coming from the red room that night. Aurora wonders if the man is moving the furniture around. But Miguel calls, so her attention is diverted.

Miguel wants to talk about the demonstration. He is exuberant, as if a victory has been won. He talks of the truckloads of police who arrived with their AK-47s and their bulletproof vests. But, he says, the throngs were not dissuaded. In the face of the enemy, the people shouted accusations. They waved their banners and called for PEACE! JUSTICE! LIBERTY! "We were the ones to beat our chests," he tells Aurora. "And the devil retreated!"

"Come home," she says. "There is a devil right here in your house."

In the morning, Lupe is still livid. In the kitchen, she bangs pots and breaks a cazuela.

"What's the matter with you?" Aurora asks.

"The man in the red room is the matter. Last night he put his big paws on me."

Aurora groans with disgust. "Animals like that should be neutered."

"Oh, no. I want the man to lose his soul, not just his huevos. So I asked the Virgen to see what she can do."

Aurora's eyes move from her Chichimeca daughter to the niche where the house virgin lives. The papier-mâché statue is draped in layers of flowery cloth to keep it warm, and Lupe has set out fresh calla lilies and lit candles in the rose-painted glasses. There is also a little pyramid of copal incense still burning there.

"But in case the Virgen is too busy," Lupe adds, "Don Antonio has his own plans."

Aurora toys with the idea of telling the man to leave as she weeds her tuberose lilies and Aztec shellflowers. But she is worried about the girl. What happens to a girl who runs into a man's fist?

At breakfast, the girl wears sunglasses, even though she is in the shade of the citrus tree and a big white umbrella. Again, she only drinks hot chocolate.

Then again, the señor is shouting into the telephone. Aurora asks him to keep his voice down; he is disturbing her customers. "My ex-wife," he says, as if these words make his action acceptable. When he joins his new wife at the table, he lights a Te Amo and does not talk to her.

Aurora does not talk to him, either. She thinks this man has a stone for a heart. She pulls the pencil out of her hair and taps her foot, then takes the man's order for sopa Azteca, which infuriates her further. This soup is only on the lunch menu and that means Lupe will have to stop everything and start chopping avocado, onion, cheese, and chile for the garnish.

When Lupe brings the soup, she puts it in front of the girl by mistake. The girl draws back, gagging on the smell of raw onion and fresh cheese. She vomits into her napkin. "I'm so sorry," she manages to say. "I'm pregnant."

After Lupe has helped the girl clean up, she says, "If you like, we can try my cure for morning sickness."

The girl goes up to lie down, and the last breakfast customers leave. A boy in Huichol dress brings his grandfather's greetings to Aurora. The boy catches the man's eye and tucks a small woven bag at the feet of the Aztec statue. When the man retrieves the bag, Aurora tells him, "Xochipili has the power to induce rapture, trance, or death. Which are you after?"

The man slips the bag into the inside pocket of his linen jacket. "Number one, of course," he replies with his movie-star smile.

The boy turns back to whisper, "No more than three or watch out for your heart."

Aurora watches the man put one peyote bud into his mouth. While she is clearing tables, she sees him eat another and then finish a third with the last of his coffee.

In a few hours, the comida rush begins. Today, the main meal includes garlic soup, avocado stuffed with shrimp, partridges in a poblano mole, and sorbet mandarina. After it is all served and cleared, Lupe and Aurora climb the stone stairs to the red room.

The girl is lying on the bed, still in her sunglasses. Aurora can see the ripple of purple at the edge of one lens. Lupe has brought a bundle of curative herbs and flowers, and she uses this like a broom to sweep up and down the girl's long, thin body. "When your blood is hot," she tells the girl, "you are nauseous and dizzy. This will cool your sickness."

While Lupe works, the man sits by the window in the animal-hide armchair, staring out at the view.

Aurora sits next to the bed and talks to the girl. "It might not be such a good idea to have your first baby in Mexico," she advises. "Maybe you should go back to the States and let your mother take care of you."

"I don't have a mother."

"I'm so sorry. When did you lose her?" Aurora asks.

"I lost two mothers," the girl says. "The one who raised me—last year. But my real mother was gone before I even knew her."

Aurora is even more alarmed for the girl. "In childbirth?" she asks.

"No. That one gave me up."

The man pops another bud into his mouth, chews it slowly, and then eats another. Aurora wonders how many he has taken in all, but she says nothing. She only hopes that something that deprives one of an appetite for food will also work on an appetite for violence.

Lupe sweeps her herbal broom back and forth across the girl's abdomen. She speaks to the embryo, addressing it as Little Quetzal Feather, as the curanderas have since Aztec times. She asks it not to give its mother such a hard battle.

The man tells Lupe her hair has turned to black feathers.

Lupe sweeps the girl with the rosemary, pepper-tree twigs, and red geraniums.

"My father's story," the girl continues, "is that a complete stranger came up to him in the street and thrust a newborn in his arms."

Aurora says, "That's hard to believe."

"His wife never believed it. But even though she was sure I was her husband's bastard, she kept me. He brought me home. She went into the bathroom and threw up; then she threw him out. That was her story, although she did take him back in the end."

"What do you believe?" Aurora asks the girl.

"Now that I'm pregnant, I can't imagine giving up a baby."

Aurora lights a cigarette and takes a deep drag. On the exhale, she says, "Giving up a child is the worst. I did this. I had a little girl who was taken from me when she was five. Perhaps that's your real mother's story—that you were taken, not given."

Last, Lupe extracts a brown egg from her apron pocket and rolls it gently up and down the girl's limbs, down the seam between her ribs and over her heart. "This is to cleanse the body," she says.

The man watches the egg's course with huge, hallucinating eyes. "Lupe holds the earth," he tells his wife, "and everywhere she rubs you, you are dirt."

Lupe takes the girl's pulse and leaves with the egg.

The man stares behind his wife at the wall of masks. He looks at them as if they are alive. His eyes shift from the bull with the flaming nostrils to the spotted, big-fanged cat to the white-horned devil. The gods appear to be talking to him, and the man begins to pant and growl back at the animal faces. Then he runs from the room.

In the kitchen, Lupe cracks the egg into a glass of water to make her diagnosis. The white rises in a whirlpool and the bubbles on the surface are dirty. She shows Aurora the glass and says, "See, a witch is at work."

Aurora does not believe in the power of brujos. She does not believe that if a witch rolls in ashes three times he can turn into a whirlwind, a comet, or even an incandescent red ball. She does not believe a witch can steal your soul for the devil. But she does know that any bad man, in his own true form, can steal everything that matters from a woman.

When Miguel calls that night, Aurora says, "There is a man in your Casa Luna who screams into the phone, a man who beats his wife, a man who will fuck anything that moves, a man who eats peyote like candy . . . We are living with a man who is an animal."

"Remember, Luz, those are his weaknesses, not his strengths."

"Come home," she repeats.

The next morning, the man asks about the bullfights.

"You may not want to go," Aurora tells the girl. "It's very bloody, and if the bull has heart, it's even worse."

Don Antonio agrees. "Let me prepare you."

There is a glint in the man's eyes as Don Antonio runs through the scenario. "First," he says, "the fat picador comes out on his armored horse to stick the bull. Then the banderillos pick at him in their magenta capes. Then the matador comes in his black horned hat to taunt the animal. He must do this for exactly seventeen minutes."

"You should know," Lupe interrupts, "in Mexico, the bull and the devil are one and the same."

"When the matador is allowed to kill," Don Antonio continues, "he aims right between the shoulder blades. But sometimes it takes a lot of tries."

"Right here?" the man asks, touching a place on his wife's back.

Before leaving for the fights, the man takes Don Antonio aside. "Can you find me the Huichole?"

"Oh, no, he comes when he feels like it."

"Can you find me some mushrooms?"

"Oh, you can buy them anywhere. Just go ask for them in the market."

In the kitchen, Aurora asks about their conversation. Don Antonio looks down at his leather sandals and explains, "A man who grabs my niece's ass belongs in jail. I am only helping him find his way."

Aurora steps out into the courtyard with the loppers to prune the white jasmine. The sun picks up the red highlights in her hair and a hummingbird hovers near by. The man and the girl leave in a green-and-white taxi.

When they return, the man is exultant. "The bull lives!" he shouts.

"Indultado?" Don Antonio asks, amazed since it is so rare that a bull has fought well enough to be pardoned.

"Oh, yes. He will spend the rest of his life eating, sleeping, and fucking. And his sons will inherit his great courage," the man says, looking pointedly at his wife.

The girl looks shaken.

Aurora asks, "And how did you survive the bulls?"

The man answers, "This time she vomited in her purse."

When Miguel calls that night, Aurora says, "Be an angel. Come home."

"She is a girl after your own heart, I see."

"Yes, and she needs your protection."

"This is your cause, Luz. You will find a way to care for your one American. I have many Mexican sisters and I cannot save the world."

"You don't believe that," Aurora snaps. "If you believed that, you would have left me in the jardín all those years ago. If you believed that, you would have left Guadalupe in the street. If you believed that for one minute, you would leave the mothers and children of Chiapas and come home."

"Yes," Miguel says. "There are so many. On every street in Mexico. And I bleed for all of them. Why don't they just tear out my heart?"

Aurora accompanies Lupe to the Tuesday market at the top of the town. First they buy the green cactus paddles for nopalitos. They buy kilos of dried beans, rice, four kinds of chiles, and fresh goat cheese. Next they stop for ripe avocados, tomatillos, tomatoes, onions, cigarettes for Aurora, a pair of knock-off Nikes for Lupe, and more bulbs for the garden. They stop to look at the caged northern birds—the cardinals, blue jays, and goldfinches. Then Lupe leads on to the sorcerers' stall, where she inspects the black chickens and the air plants used for cures, and picks through the brujo's bags of twigs, roots, leaves, and dried flowers. She buys some coyote fat for Aurora's arthritis.

The brujo also has a good assortment of milagros for miraculous healings. There are little tin eyes and legs to pin with prayers to the Madonna's dress. There is a milagro for every body part, but only the hearts come in super size. It appears that, more than anything else, people are sick at heart.

Aurora notices the bad man at the next stall, which sells paraphernalia for bullfighters and their fans. The man is buying an espada.

"Where is your wife?" Aurora calls to him.

"Again, not feeling well." The man asks Lupe sarcastically if she has any more cures.

"Right here," Lupe says.

The man runs his finger along the blade one more time, waits for his sword to be wrapped in newspaper, then joins the women.

His proximity makes Aurora's skin crawl. She hates this man. He fingers the small packets that promise sexual ecstasy and Aurora wants to slap his hands. She tells him, "Foreigners are supposed to be immune to Mexican magic." The brujo suggests a love charm. "If you want a lot of women," Aurora translates, "wear it in your sock."

The man pays the brujo, tucks the amulet in his shoe, points to Lupe's chest, and asks, "Where can I get some mangoes like those?"

The brujo, who seems to think the man wants to win Lupe's heart, points to his biggest milagro, which is engulfed in flames and backed by the cross.

When Lupe gets back to the Casa Luna she scrapes all the spines off the fresh cactus paddles and goes to plant them in the man's shorts.

She searches the red room, but she can't find any of his clothes. "It appears he only has the one suit," she tells Aurora. "No spare underwear, either."

"Yes, I heard him on the phone. His ex-wife has apparently chosen to give his clothes away instead of shipping them."

"The girl has clothes, though, and some are stained with blood . . . not a good sign for that baby of hers."

On Sunday evening, Aurora watches the paseo from her balcony. The pretty young mestizas promenade around the jardín in one direction; their male admirers pass them going the other way. The only illumination comes from the paper lanterns that hang from the trees, but Aurora can tell they are flashing their eyes at each other. She watches an exchange between a swaggering charro, still in his chaps and spurs, and the prettiest girl whose black bangs have been curled out and under on a giant roller. A mariachi band strolls by them, hoping this cowboy will pay for a serenade. But although the mestiza has taken his red neckerchief, she moves along with her girlfriends in the opposite direction.

Later on, Aurora spots the man from the red room. He is sitting next to the mestiza with the big bangs. Aurora sees him work his charm. She imagines the mestiza is thinking, *This may be the man who will take me away from this town. Yes, this man could put me in a big white house. Maybe he will even get me a part in a movie. . . .* Aurora sees the man whisper in her ear. She sees the mestiza turn away. She sees the man tear the red neckerchief from her throat and retie it under his own collar. She sees the man take hold of the mestiza and pull her to her feet.

Aurora wants to shout "No!" from her balcony, but the word stays in her mouth along with her heart.

When Miguel calls, he scoffs at her fears. "The man is just posturing. He tries on the devil's clothes, and you think he has power, but it is only a guise. Just tell him that people won't stand for this."

"It is not so easy," Aurora replies. "For God's sake, Miguel. Be a saint. Come home."

The man does not come home that night, either.

The next morning, Lupe hangs a cross of fresh marigolds above the big wooden door. This is to keep the devil away.

When the man walks under the cross at ten, his eyes are bloodshot, his suit is rumpled, and his chin is whiskered. He nods to Aurora and she nods back, but she wants to hit him with the stick she uses to break open the piñatas.

She tours her garden because this calms her. She deadheads the spent flowers and tosses them in a basket for Lupe's teas.

When Don Antonio arrives, his face is red with anger. He tells Aurora, "The man in the white linen suit has raped my brother's daughter."

"Raped?" Aurora whispers.

"There are only good girls in my family. They would never say yes. I tell you . . . ese señor is the devil's slave."

"Report him."

"To the police? My word against the gringo's?" Don Antonio asks laughing. "No, it will be more effective if I report him to the ancestors."

In the mail, there is a poem from Miguel. In it he tells Aurora to put on the saint's clothes herself. "I give you the heavenly mantle," he writes. "Here is the feathered helmet. And the golden wings. Dress up, my Luz. That is not so hard. That is all a man does."

There is also a small parcel for the man. He tears it open, throws it to the ground, and stomps on it as if to kill a scorpion.

The next day, the man throws open his doors, steps onto his balcony, and shouts down at Aurora, "I found one of my shoes in the bathtub, and my name is written on the bottom of it."

"How about that?" Aurora shouts back. "Do you know what day it is?"

"Friday," he spits impatiently.

"Yes. The witches work on both Tuesdays and Fridays."

That night Aurora is even more uneasy. Casa Luna's stone walls are two feet thick, but still, she hears loud, muffled noises emerging from the red room. She knocks on the door and no one answers, but it is quiet after that. She climbs another flight to the starlight lounge, lies on the couch by the bar, and tries to unwind with a cigarette. She props her head up

on embroidered pillows and watches the flight of a night moth. It has
four shining triangles marked on its huge, dark wings, and it is called the
Butterfly of Knives, after the Aztec deity most fond of bloody hearts.

When Miguel calls, Aurora tells him, "The man has bought a
sword. Go to your revolutionaries and get the girl a gun."

"You would make the better soldadera, my Luz. The girl doesn't
know yet that she can protect herself. But you know about independence. You know because it is the same long story again. Finish your
story, Luz, and I will be home before you know it."

The next morning, Lupe picks some black, malodorous seeds from the
angel trumpet tree and grinds them in a mortar. When Aurora asks for
an explanation, Lupe says, "My aunt married a man who beat her.
When she'd had enough, she started lacing his coffee with toloache, and
the man became weak and humble and always kept his head down."

"You better know what you're doing," Aurora warns.

"It can deaden the testicles, too," Lupe adds, putting a pinch of the
powder into a cup before pouring the coffee and bringing it to the man
with his huevos revueltos. When she returns, she tells Aurora, "My aunt
is the queen now, and the man is her servant."

The girl does not come down until noon. She orders caldo tlapeño, a
special chicken soup, but when it comes, she only plays with her spoon.
It is very hot out, yet she is wearing a long-sleeved dress and sunglasses
in the shade.

Aurora comes to refill the man's coffee. The man tells his wife to
remove her glasses. She shakes her head, meaning no. Suddenly he looks
like he has eaten a jaguar for breakfast, and she gives in. The bruise has
turned a yellowish green. Aurora is so angry that she stares right into
the man's eyes and says, "You are correct in thinking a certain amount
of wife beating is accepted in Mexico . . . but there are limits—especially if a woman is carrying a child!"

The man puts his head back and howls with laughter. "Do you
really think I'd tell her to take her glasses off if I had done that?" He
yawns and goes back to the red room for his siesta.

This surprises Aurora because she knows the man doesn't like to let the girl out of his sight. She takes advantage of his absence and asks the girl if she would like to go to the agua mágica, the hot springs just outside of town. The girl seems nervous but she gets in the Volkswagen Beetle anyway. They climb up the cobbled streets and then head west past scattered stucco huts, junked cars, and a few roadside stands selling lead-glazed pottery, old wagons, and fake antiques.

At La Gruta, there is a series of pools that get progressively hotter. In the parking lot, there is a big cat with spotted fur and dark bands around its tail. It is hunkered over something visceral, but it lets them go by. When they emerge from the changing room, it is waiting outside, but again, it lets them pass.

The girl takes off her towel to slip into the first pool. For a moment, Aurora can see four cuts, made at regular intervals up the girl's forearm, as if someone had been trying to slice a loaf of bread. She gasps and says, "What happened to you?"

"It's nothing," the girl says, quickly winding her long hair into a bun. "I just got into some cactus spines, that's all."

Aurora knows that thorns puncture skin, leaving red circular marks, not slices, but all she says is, "Wounds can go septic here. You should let Lupe give you some ointment for that."

The girl has sunken in up to her shoulders, so all Aurora can see now is her head. They soak in the warm water, floating on their backs and resting their necks against the stone wall. Aurora asks, "Tell me, how long have you known your husband?"

"Not long."

"How long is that?"

The girl rewinds her hair, and says, "It's been two months since I ran away."

"Ran away from whom?"

The girl kicks her long legs and swims toward the next pool. Aurora swims behind her. When they reach the hotter water, the girl swims in place. "When my mom died, I wasn't eighteen yet, so I had to stay with my father. That was really not a good scene. Not only did my father have a problem with me, he had a problem with my boyfriend, and when I got pregnant, he had a problem with that, too . . . and, well, so did my boyfriend. So I guess you'd say I ran away from both of them."

They are swimming in the tunnel now which leads to the last and hottest pool. The passage is dark and narrow and otherworldly. Halfway through, the girl starts to panic. Aurora has to tell her three times to stand up before the girl stops flailing and puts her feet down. The water comes halfway up her ribs, and Aurora takes her hand and walks her the rest of the way into the steamy, round grotto.

Through holes in the ceiling, light pours down like god rays on the girl who is lying on a central stone platform. The baby is not showing yet, although Aurora thinks she is probably shapelier than she usually is. The girl catches Aurora looking at her, and says, "I've never had breasts before, but my husband hasn't a clue."

"So," Aurora asks, "What was next?"

"I hitchhiked to Colorado and got a job in a coffee house."

The girl seems to have stopped talking, so Aurora fills in the blanks. "You had a whirlwind romance," she prompts, ". . . with an older man . . . and then you married him . . ."

"He was already married, so I refused to have anything to do with him."

"But he won you in the end . . ."

"He was very charming. He had money. I was already pregnant. And for some reason, he was really fixated on me. He got a quickie divorce, and the next thing I knew I was running away with him."

"Does he think the child is his?"

"No," she says turning over to steam on her stomach. "He's definitely done the math."

Aurora swims to stand under the waterfall on one side of the cave. It pours down with such force that it feels as if someone is beating her with fists. When the girl moves in to take her turn, she cringes under the violent onslaught and quickly swims out of its range.

On the way back to Casa Luna, Aurora says, "Listen, I know what it's like to be in the power of a man." She tries to draw the girl out further, but her replies are cryptic. As the twilight transforms the landscape, the girl wants to talk about how the canyon-riddled mountains look like they have muscles, how the bulls in the corrals look stronger than God, how the maguey plants look like giant grabbing hands, how the sun looks like a bloody streak on the horizon. What she doesn't notice is how a bobcat has cut through the chaparral and is shadowing them home.

The man is not at Casa Luna. Don Antonio is digging a pit in the garden.

Aurora tells him they saw a bobcat three times in one afternoon. Don Antonio says, "If the ancestors believe a person is behaving badly, they let his animal spirit out of the corral and into the world."

It is getting pretty dark, but Aurora can see him put the shovel down and pick up a sack. He takes out what appears to be a clay man. It has a hole in its stomach, and Don Antonio inserts the stub of a candle—the kind that is used at wakes. He dresses the image in two pieces of white linen and ties some blonde hair to the head. Then he buries it. When he's done, he brushes off his hands and says with a shrug, "I've given the Virgin two new dresses and a silver crown. She will forgive me."

Aurora is a bit spooked. In the eerie light, she drinks two shots of tequila and has three cigarettes in quick succession before going up to bed, again without the comfort of her lover.

In the late morning, the man comes home. A pocket is missing from his jacket and a cuff off his pants. He asks for coffee and sits next to the girl by the orange tree. Again, Lupe puts a pinch of Datura seed in his cup.

Soon the Huichole comes with another small bag. He plants it by the statue. Once the man has retrieved it, the Indian sits at his table. "Nanacat," he pronounces as the man surreptitiously puzzles over the round-headed, long-stemmed fungi. The Huichole tells him to eat the mushrooms with honey or they will burn his mouth and throat.

The man gives Lupe a big wink and asks her to bring some honey to his room. Lupe refuses, so Don Antonio follows after the man with the honeycomb from the Sierra Madre Mountains.

Aurora brings the Huichole a plate of chiles en nogada, stuffed peppers in a walnut sauce. "If you eat more than three," the Huichole warns, "terrifying things will appear. Because of this, some men hang themselves. And some fling themselves from balconies," he says with a glance toward the red room. "Some have a change of heart."

Aurora sets a Coca-Cola next to the Indian and says, "Thank you for looking after this house." When Don Antonio returns, he tells the girl she is wanted upstairs.

After he finishes his meal, the Huichole helps Aurora in her garden. They are both listening, but there are no sounds coming from the red room.

It is dusk before they see the man again. He stumbles through the courtyard, but before he goes out into the street, he looks accusingly at Aurora and says, "There are scorpions in my room."

"Do you think it's the mushrooms talking?" she asks the Huichole.

"A scorpion in a man's vision is a sign of lechery," he says. "It can also predict destruction and death." He reaches into a big cloth bag and places a gun by the Prince of Flowers. Then the belt of bullets. It is after nine when he says good night.

Aurora thanks him again for looking after her house and goes to see about the girl and the scorpions.

When she knocks, there is no answer. She bangs louder and calls the girl's name. Still, there is no answer. She asks Lupe for the other key, but it turns out the man had requested the spare yesterday, saying he'd lost the first.

Aurora has Don Antonio unscrew the hinges.

The girl is a ghostly white. There is a red neckerchief stuffed in her mouth. Her hands are tied to the headboard. She is also tied by her hair to the ironwork. The girl is black and blue around her ribs and the sheet is bloody from a slash between her shoulder blades.

When they unbind her, she rears up in a rage. She is punching at the air, at the pillows, at the hands that reach out to soothe her.

When they ungag her, she begins her screaming. "No more!" is what she yells. And then she is sobbing.

"Yes, enough," Aurora says. "¡Ya Basta!"

As per Lupe's instructions, Don Antonio leaves to steep flowers for a sedative tea. Aurora tries to calm the girl and Lupe applies cold compresses to the bruises and tapes the wound. By the time Don Antonio returns with the steaming pot, they have wrapped the weeping girl in a white cotton dress. Aurora spoons the tea into the girl, and on the graves of his ancestors, Don Antonio swears the señor will not be back. Finally, the girl sleeps.

Aurora retrieves the gun and the bandoleer from its hiding spot by Xochipili's feet, and sits down to wait under the girl's balcony. Don Antonio also stands watch in the dark courtyard. "The gun suits you," he tells Aurora. "You look like our Adelita."

"And who was she?"

"Of course you know her; she was a famous fighter in our struggle for independence."

"Well, it makes me feel strong, anyway," Aurora says, putting one hand under the barrel and the other on the trigger. But she realizes it is not just the gun. It is also Lupe's Virgin, Don Antonio's ancestors, and the Aztec Prince of Flowers who empower her. It's Miguel's verse and the Huichole's vision. But the real reason she can stand in the way of a bad man is because of the girl who has said "No more."

Yes, she will do this for Hallie, the girl. Also for the cousin with the big bangs. For Lupe, her child of the Chichimeca. For Molly, the child of her own body. For La Llorona, the Aztec's weeping woman. And for La Luz del Norte—yes, for herself, she will do this. She will stop the man who likes the blood of young girls.

There are noises in the street. Then there is a loud crash across the courtyard. Aurora stands at attention, ready to bar the man's entry, but Don Antonio grabs the gun out of her hands, switches off the safety and fires at a fleet, black shadow. There is a scream. And the rattle and rush of a soul leaving a body.

They approach the spot cautiously. A pottery urn has broken to pieces. And under the jacaranda vine, a bobcat is dead.

"If a man's animal spirit is killed," Don Antonio pronounces very soberly, "the man himself will die." He hands the shotgun to Aurora, slings the big cat over his shoulder and leaves to bury the dead animal.

There is more commotion in the street, but Aurora does not open the big wooden door. Whoever comes will have to first face the carving of the warrior angel, and then they will have to face her. She goes back to her post to wait.

Aurora wakes at dawn to the sound of someone's fist on this door. The voice she hears is not the man's, and when it identifies itself, she hides the gun by the statue and then greets the policeman.

Over the din of the neighbor's rooster, he asks for the wife of James Harkness, the Señora Hallie.

Aurora asks, "What has happened?"

"The man is dead."

Don Antonio appears, wiping the sleep from his eyes, and Aurora sends him up to the red room for the girl.

"How?" Aurora asks the lieutenant.

"We are still investigating. There are people who say they heard a shot, but there is no bullet in the man's body."

"You think it's a homicide?"

"Perhaps."

"Where did it happen?"

"Just outside your wall there," he says pointing across the courtyard by the jacaranda vine.

"Have you any ideas, Señora?"

Don Antonio returns running. "The girl is gone . . . the Señora Hallie is gone," he says.

"That makes Señora Hallie a suspect," the lieutenant says, as he accepts a cup of coffee from Lupe and adds three lumps of brown sugar.

"What time did the man die?" Aurora asks.

"Around midnight."

"Hallie was here. There are three of us who can swear to that."

"She has only run away," Lupe says.

"From a dead man?" the policeman asks.

Don Antonio interrupts, "Is it a crime, Lieutenant, just to wish a man dead?"

"What are you getting at?"

"Some people blame witchcraft for your unsolved crimes."

"There is no such thing," the lieutenant replies, "but if there was, a witch would not go after this man. He had a big heart. He was giving away money in the streets last night. They say he was weeping openly for the poor women. He was crying for the children. This is what the eyewitnesses say."

Aurora says, "We can't be talking about the same man."

"Perhaps it was the magic mushrooms," the Huichole says. "Such a change of heart can come from a vision. Also, a suicide."

Aurora is surprised to see the Indian sitting at a table, having no idea how or when he had returned to the Casa Luna.

"Drugs?" the policeman asks, "What can you tell me, Indian?"

Just then, Miguel Hernández walks through the doorway into his courtyard. "I have heard about the tragedy," he says quickly, putting his leather bag down to shake the lieutenant's hand and embrace Aurora. "You should hear the stories they are telling in the street. Already this man has become a legend." Miguel takes a moment to run his fingers through his hair, but he continues to command everyone's respectful attention. "The people are calling him 'The Waterfall,' " Miguel goes on. "They tell me that tears poured out of his eyes and pesos poured out of his hands. A hundred times, they say, the man reached into his silver-lined pockets and filled the palms of the poor."

"But the beggar in a blue rebozo . . ." the lieutenant adds, ". . . the Chichimeca who sells the dolls . . . you know the one, Señor, just outside your door . . ."

"Yes?" Lupe asks.

"She was the last to see his money. The man handed her a hundred-peso note and she spat on it."

"As I thought," Don Antonio mutters.

"But you know, Lieutenant," Miguel says, stroking his Zapata-like mustache, "I would point the finger at natural causes, not homicide or suicide. It seems much more likely that the man has died of a heart attack."

"Yes, a heart attack," the policeman repeats, following Miguel Hernández to the table by the orange tree and accepting his invitation to the best breakfast in town.

LA DEL SAPO

Karleen Pendleton Jiménez

In memory of Doña Tomasa
190?–2000

NAMING IS NOTHING NEW. IT IS POSSESSION. I COULD LIVE ALONE on an island thousands of miles away from civilization, and if you found me, the first thing you would do is name me, even if I look nothing like anyone you've ever seen or maybe precisely because of that. It has never been about distinguishing difference. It's about control.

Ara's mother returned as a wealthy woman to her hometown a half century after she left with a single suitcase of clothing and pictures. She is very proud of this fact. She had married a hardworking farmer and never wasted a single kernel of corn. She never lived extravagantly. Even at ninety-two, she won't spend the twenty dollars needed for a taxicab to visit her favorite church in the neighboring town. She will, however, release thousands of dollars every month to the local priest, much to the irritation of her daughter. But nobody, not even Ara, mistakes this money as a simple act of faith or selflessness. When the church bells

ring, we all smile at each other across the table. Those are her bells.
They ring when she wants them to. When the town voted to change the
time a year ago to stay consistent with the rest of the state, she voiced
her disapproval. The priest, shortly after, decided to keep the local mass
at her requested hour. In fact, everyone entering or leaving the house
and garden of Doña Tomasa does so in accordance with her specific
time zone.

Doña Tomasa has named each of Ara's girlfriends according to
characteristics or appearance. The last girlfriend to visit was named "La
Cansada" (the tired one). She acquired this name while failing to keep
up with the task of grinding corn for tamales. I had decided long
before I got on the plane to Guadalajara that I would build the muscles to succeed at this task. Let's face it, no self-respecting butch could
live with that name or the knowledge that this ninety-two-year-old
woman still grinds her own corn without incident. Never mind that an
electric corn grinder sits covered only a few feet from where my muscles burned.

It rains every afternoon during the summers in this tropical town
which rests in the greenest valley of México. The air thickens, thunder
pounds, the birdcage is covered, and my girlfriend and I sneak upstairs
to the balcony outside her bedroom and kiss. An hour or so later, after
we have made love and the storm has passed, we return downstairs to
the patio and Doña Tomasa wakening from her nap. We are not alone.
The wet and electricity motivate a variety of frogs to play in her garden.
One or two boldly join us on the patio only to be promptly scooped
and thrown back into the dirt. "Qué cochinos," Doña Tomasa grum-
bles as they fly. "They're lucky they're still small," Ara grins at me while
washing the corn husk. "She doesn't like frogs."

On the first morning in México, the three-year-old neighbor boy
(named Doro within the perimeter of Doña Tomasa's household and
Rodrigo everywhere else) giggled in her arms as she whispered to him.
Her hand slipped down his crotch and he screamed with happiness or
fear or both. It was impossible to tell which and I couldn't make out her
words. After a few minutes of this routine, I asked Ara what she was saying to him.

She looks up from the dishes and laughs. "She asked him if el sapo (the frog) has come and taken his 'manhood' away. He assures her that it hasn't, but she says she doesn't believe him. Normally, when we're not here, he'll take it out for her to prove it." My face wrinkles around the ouch forming in my mouth. I instinctively cover my own crotch. "I'm afraid of the frogs here."

Following classic lesbian tradition, I grew up mistaken as a boy and have never grown out of it. My girlfriend and I are both quite aware that I am a woman, but we always kid around with the idea of an imaginary "manhood" pressed under my jeans. Or then again, maybe there was more to this frog story than I wanted to know. Possible explanations? . . . No, no it was getting too creepy to think about. Especially after Sunday mass when Doña Tomasa had decided that I was in fact a boy.

"Look at her haircut, Ara, that's a perfect man's haircut. That's what I've been trying to get for the boys next door all year." Sitting on her little wooden bench, yes, *her* little wooden bench (anyone else needs permission to join her), she had the perfect view of Doro, his brother Luis, and me. Later, she would sneak comments to Ara in the kitchen when I would get up to clear the dishes. "I'm telling you, I look at her from the front and I look at her from the back, and she's a boy." Ara tried to assure her otherwise, but she was unconvinced. I started to panic. I'd seen her grab the boy, and Ara had herself been goosed coming downstairs after a storm, as a gesture of affection I had guessed, but neither of us was sure. I was certain, though, that either her curiosity would get the better of her and her sturdy wrinkled hand would find me, or that these frogs at some point would attack. It got to be that upon re-entering the kitchen or finding Ara and her mother together at the table working, they would start giggling together about "el sapo," and I would again cross my hands over my crotch, which would make them laugh even harder.

"I have always been afraid of my mother," Ara tells me after Luis spills his juice and Doña Tomasa yells about learning responsibility. "There is no talking during meals, no getting up for the bathroom or the front door, and definitely no spilling," Ara whispers as we sip quietly at our soup. I eat second helpings of everything she makes, wash the dishes immediately after dinner, keep the kids quiet when she's praying, and take everyone out to play on the street when she needs to be alone. I am trying to score major points with the mother-in-law, but I admit to Ara that I am also afraid of her. She winks back at me and answers, "And that's all she really wants."

On our last evening in México, we hear a noise outside while sipping Doña Tomasa's café con leche in the kitchen. The old lady gets up and goes out to the patio. We hear her curse something about cochinos and sapos and jump up to look. Sitting in her shovel is a large bright-eyed frog. "Oh no," my girlfriend shakes her head slowly, "Don't look."

"Why, what's gonna happen? You gotta tell me," I say anxiously.

"I told you she doesn't like frogs. She'll kill it. Very slow. Acid."

❧ ⊱━━⊰ ❧

I escaped the next day from her curious fingers and el sapo, but I was much luckier than that frog. Every Sunday since, Ara has called her mother and they talk and laugh, and Doña Tomasa always makes a point of telling her to say hi to "La del Sapo" (she of the frog), my new name.

THE PLUMED SERPENT
OF LOS ANGELES

Daniel A. Olivas

I KNOW YOUR PARENTS, BEING GOOD MEXICANS, TAUGHT YOU THAT although Columbus came from Italy, the Spanish crown commissioned his voyage to El Nuevo Mundo and so his three ships sailed under a Spanish flag. Then, a bit later, Spanish conquistadors and missionaries with names like Hernando Cortés and Friar Bartolomé de las Casas and Álvar Núñez Cabeza de Vaca came and, as that son-of-a-bitch Cromwell did to the Irish, they liberated the native people of their "barbarian" pagan beliefs and gave them Catholicism. Or so the Spanish conquistadors and missionaries thought. For, as we say in Spanish: "La zorra mudará los dientes mas no las mientes." A fox might lose its teeth, but not its nature. Therefore, just because the Spanish banished the old Aztec gods so that the people had to worship in churches, they forgot to ask the gods if they wanted to leave. In other words, because the Spanish forgot their manners, the old Aztec gods hung around and did what they could to make mischief in the lives of the mestizos—the new people of mixed Spanish and Indian blood—so that they would never forget who were the true ruling powers of the land.

The same is true in Ireland: the ancient gods still rumble through the night or pop up on a spring morning and cause mischief on that beautiful green island. I know this because, believe it or not, I have traveled throughout Ireland. When I was much younger, I hitchhiked through most of that wonderful island (I stayed in the south of Ireland because I was too nervous to deal with the shooting up north!) and on more than one occasion, I saw the mischief of the old Celtic gods. Little things, sometimes. Like when I was having beer at a pub in Galway on the western coast—a nice pint of Guinness—and I looked up at the wall by the dartboard and saw a painting. It was a typical painting of Ireland's patron saints: John Fitzgerald Kennedy, his brother Robert, and the Pope. Well, just as I was staring at the painting, admiring its workmanship, in a blink, the painting changed! Now, instead of John Fitzgerald Kennedy, his brother Robert, and the Pope, I saw, clear as day, John Fitzgerald Kennedy, his brother Robert, and *Muhammad Ali!* The greatest boxer who ever entered a ring! Float like a mariposa, sting like an abeja! I looked around the pub and no one else was looking and I wanted to yell "¡Chingada!" but I just stood there, mouth agape like a pinche pendejo, clenching my pint of Guinness. But there he was, clear as an Arizona morning, Muhammad Ali, the former Mr. Cassius Marcellas Clay, smiling that little sly smile of his and looking at me with that twinkle in his eyes that he used to have—before he got sick and started shaking—you know, when he used to appear on *The Mike Douglas Show*, and tease him something bad because it looked like he didn't know how to act around Black folk. That magical transformation of the painting on that pub's wall in Galway—that, mis amigos, was the work of a pinche Irish god!

Well, the old Aztec gods are just as bad. No, worse! ¡Ay Dios mío! Don't get me wrong. They won't kill or anything. But their idea of a joke can sometimes include a little physical and emotional pain. And they don't care who their next victim is. So, when the Spanish came, the old gods went underground and hid during the daylight but, when it got dark, they came back up to play their tricks on the mestizos and Indians. But this is where my story begins: the most pissed off Aztec god was—who else?—Quetzalcoatl. Just like Ali, he was simply the greatest, and he ruled the Aztecs and the Toltecs with an iron fist. His fame continued even into the twentieth century when D. H. Lawrence—one of my favorite writers; you know, he's buried in Taos, New Mexico—wrote a novel and called it *Quetzalcoatl*. But his publishers were worried that with such a strange title the book wouldn't sell so they changed it to *The Plumed Serpent*. Because that's what Quetzalcoatl was: a snake with many beautiful feathers surrounding his face. Few would condemn me for saying that Quetzalcoatl was probably the greatest god the Americas have ever known.

Now, Quetzi—as his friends called him because, let's face it, even for gods, "Quetzalcoatl" is quite a mouthful—Quetzi was a grouchy son-of-a-bitch because, well, you would be too if you were a great god and then the Spanish told your people to worship Jesus Christ, and they do—can you believe it!—they do. This Jesus, fumed Quetzi, doesn't require human sacrifices! Hell, he let *himself* be sacrificed! What kind of god does that? And then, to top it off, other people, pale people, come and take over the land you once ruled.

Most of the other Aztec gods took on human form the way you would if you were in their position. Gods with names like Huitzilopochtli, Chalchihuitlicue, and Tlacahuepan became José, María, and Hernán. They looked at the human population and found the best-looking examples of humanity that they could. Sometimes they mixed and matched different features. But they chose good-looking hombres y damas and transmuted into these beautiful people! The best-looking faces and legs and arms and man-oh-Manischewitz! They were the best-looking Mexicans you ever saw with skin as smooth and brown as polished Indian pottery with raven black hair that glistened in the sun! And, at night, only at night, well after midnight, they changed back into their original forms and flew through Mexico and played their evil tricks on the poor unsuspecting, Jesus-worshipping mestizos and Indians.

But Quetzi was so angry that he left Tenochtitlán—you know, Mexico City—and wandered without purpose for almost three hundred years. He eventually headed north until he found a little one-room hut far from his home in a place that would eventually be called El

Pueblo de Nuestra Señora la Reina de los Ángeles de la Porciúncula now known simply as "Los Angeles." You see, he had suffered greatly once before and this latest insult was too much for him to bear. It is a painful and embarrassing story, but you must know it to understand why Quetzi could not live in his home of Tenochtitlán anymore. Centuries before the Spanish came, the god Tezcatlipoca disguised himself as a great hairy spider and offered Quetzi his very first taste of pulque which—as I'm sure you know—is much stronger than tequila. *Oh!* That shit will get you borracho! And Quetzi loved the feeling he got from the pulque and drank so much that, in a drunken heat, he had his way with his sister, Quetzalpetlatl! The *shame* of it! So, Quetzi banished himself and wandered the land for many generations.

But this Spanish conquest thing, that was too much for Quetzi to stomach. So, as I said, Quetzi left Tenochtitlán and eventually ended up in old Los Angeles living in a little adobe hut. And, in his disgust, instead of choosing a beautiful body to transmute into, Quetzi borrowed the looks of the first person he saw after the Spanish banned the Aztec religion. Unfortunately, the first person he laid his eyes on was a broken-down old borrachín who was bald as a mango with a large pot of a belly that hung below his belt. But Quetzi's anger blinded him so that he didn't care.

One day, poor old Quetzi left his little adobe to look for something to eat. Yes, he now suffered from hunger of the human type. So he headed to the little hut owned by this vieja, an old Indian woman who bartered with anyone who wanted good Mexican comida and who had something she might want. But, as he scrambled down some rocks to avoid taking the long way on the foot-worn dirt road, the stupid Aztec god tripped on his own feet and landed with a THUMP! right in the scrubby bushes. You see, the drunkard that Quetzi turned into had these goddamn big Godzilla-like feet, so it was easy to trip just walking.

Suddenly, as he lay there with a spinning head, Quetzi noticed a woman standing over him. A beautiful woman! And for a moment, his bitterness and grouchiness melted away and he felt a little joy in his rock of a heart.

"Quetzalcoatl?" the woman said.

Goddamn! Quetzi thought. This beautiful human knows my name!

"Quetzalcoatl?" the woman said again, this time with urgency in her voice. Before he could answer, the woman said, "We need you. We need you now!"

"Who?" said Quetzi rubbing his nalgas as he stood up with the help of the beautiful woman.

"We do. The old Aztec gods. We need you!"

And at that moment, Quetzi recognized the beautiful woman's eyes. The rest of her face, he did not know, but he knew the eyes of his sister, Quetzalpetlatl, the one whom he had disgraced so many years before. But he suddenly grew angry and growled, "Go to hell!" He dusted himself off and got onto the main dirt road. But she followed him.

"Please, O great Quetzalcoatl! Our way of life is being threatened and we need all the power of the old days to survive, to win! Please don't run from me!" The beautiful woman had great tears falling from her eyes as she almost ran by Quetzi's side.

Quetzi suddenly stopped and turned to the beautiful woman. His face burned a deep red and he sputtered, "Where were my compañeros and compañeras when the Spanish came to banish us? Huh? Where?"

Quetzalpetlatl looked down, ashamed. Quetzi continued: "You did not fight then, did you? I asked you all to fight but you goddamn cowards just hid and let Jesus and Mary and Joseph and all those pinche saints replace us! You cowards! Leave me be! Do I look like a pendejo to you?" And with that, Quetzi started to walk with a quick gait, kicking up dust and rocks.

Quetzalpetlatl thought for a moment and, in a panic, she said, "If we win, you can rule all of us again! I promise!"

And, this, my friends, made Quetzi stop and think. Oh, to be the highest god again! Could he even remember how it felt? Quetzi looked out to the clear Los Angeles sky. He trained his eyes on a hawk circling on the eastern horizon.

Quetzalpetlatl saw that her brother considered the possibilities. So, to up the ante, she added, "And I will forgive you, and you will no longer carry shame in your heart."

Oh, joy! thought Quetzi. Can I have it all again? Is it possible? But it has to be done the right way. So Quetzi said, "Let's go and get some food, mi hermana, and talk about what is needed."

They found their way to the little hut owned by the old Indian woman to get something to eat. Quetzi's sister offered the vieja beautiful stones and, in exchange, received two wooden platters of pollo in a thick mole sauce and a large, steaming pile of corn tortillas wrapped in a moist towel. They then found a nice place to sit under a large pine tree so that Quetzi could learn what was afoot.

Quetzi's sister explained that the Christian god of evil, Satan, had decided to set up shop in the various cities and towns of the Americas. Satan, being legion, sent parts of himself throughout the land to lay the foundation for a revolution, to displace Jesus and rule the human race. But in order to topple Christianity, he also had to purge the land of the Aztec gods. A clean slate, he wanted. A complete coup. And the first place Satan was going to go was to El Pueblo de Nuestra Señora la Reina de los Ángeles de la Porciúncula. You see, Satan appreciated irony and what better place to begin than a pueblo named after Jesus' mother? As I told you, Satan is legion, so he sent the female part of himself, La Diabla, to plan the war against the old Aztec gods. La Diabla, it was learned, found a little cave in Malibu by the ocean and there she plotted.

"So," said Quetzi as he wiped mole from his round face with his already filthy sleeve, "all we have to do is kill La Diabla. Right?"

His sister thought for a moment and then said, "No, La Diabla cannot be killed. But she can be weakened. She can be taught a lesson. La Diabla can be seduced." As she said this last thing, she looked down and blushed a dark red-brown.

"Ah," said Quetzi, purposely ignoring his sister's embarrassment. "We must be clever." And then he laughed. "Why don't we pull that pulque trick Tezcatlipoca pulled on me all those years ago and get La Diabla muy borracha!" Quetzi let out a big laugh and then a loud fart, not caring because, after all, he had lived as an anchorite in his little hut for so long that his manners were atrocious.

"Perhaps," said Quetzalpetlatl, covering her nose as nonchalantly as possible. "But we must get you in shape first."

Quetzi looked down at himself and saw what she meant. He had chosen a poor example of a human form. But he felt needed again and said, "I'll do whatever you need me to do!"

So it began on that day. Quetzalpetlatl became her brother's own personal trainer. And for two months, she made Quetzi run and eat small meals and lift large stones in the heat of the desert day and stop drinking booze. At the end of two months, Quetzi's belly grew flat and strong and his face burned a nice healthy brown and his arms and legs developed bands of pulsating muscles. And, my friends, while they were getting Quetzi in shape, they started to develop a plan, step by step, always trying to remember La Diabla's psychology.

In getting Quetzi in shape, his sister couldn't do anything about his bald head—he was a total pelón! But Quetzi allowed his beard to grow and his sister then trimmed it into a fine mustache and goatee. Quetzalpetlatl helped her brother find beautiful clothes to show off his new physique. She stood him in front of a mirror in his little hut and they both admired his new physical power. Poor Quetzalpetlatl felt ashamed because she admired her brother in all his manliness, but she shook herself from within and said, "You are now ready to seduce La Diabla and save us!"

As I've told you, La Diabla could not be killed but her power could be limited, tied in knots. And she loved bargains. It's funny. La Diabla is vicious and evil but she always keeps a bargain. The trick, though, is to lure her into a bargain that will backfire and, to do that, you have to rely on her weakness: her pride. Remember, pride led Satan to be cast from heaven in the first place. And as they say in America, you can't teach an old dog new tricks! So they hatched a plan whereby Quetzi would challenge La Diabla to a duel of sorts. A duel of gods. If La Diabla won, the Aztec gods would leave this world without protest. But if Quetzi prevailed, La Diabla would leave the Americas forever and use the rest of the world for her playground.

But first, Quetzi had to go to Malibu where La Diabla lived. His sister bargained for a great stallion and a fine saddle and Quetzi prepared for his twenty-six mile trek to the coast. When all was prepared, Quetzalpetlatl helped Quetzi mount the magnificent horse. She said, "I love you, my brother."

"And I you," said Quetzi proudly as he dug his spurs into the horse and headed west.

Now, the Chumash Indians still lived by the beach and, indeed, they named it "umalido," which means "where the surf is loud," which eventually became "Malibu." As Quetzi came within a few miles of La Diabla's cave, the Chumash looked up from their daily lives and stared in amazement at the striking figure cut by the newly minted hero-to-be. As he neared La Diabla's home, Quetzi's nostrils filled with the stench of evil and his horse became skittish.

"There, there, my beauty," said Quetzi in a soothing voice as he patted his horse's muscular neck. "All will be well." The horse slowly calmed and continued its march toward the profane shelter. When they reached the mouth of the cave, Quetzi could see nothing but black, so he dismounted and pulled a lantern from the side of his saddle and lit it. Slowly, wary of the rocky ground, Quetzi entered the cave. He walked, one foot gently placed in front of the other, for almost an hour. What the hell am I doing? he thought. What will become of me? The darkness of the cave almost swallowed the flickering light of the lantern.

Suddenly, Quetzi stopped with a crunch of gravel under his shining boots. He sensed a presence, though no figure appeared.

"What took you so long?" said an unseen woman.

The skin on Quetzi's bald head danced with fear. He sucked in as much air as possible and said, "It is I, the great Quetzalcoatl! Come out so that I may see you, Diabla!"

And he got his wish. Without a sound, La Diabla appeared before Quetzi. I cannot describe her other than to say that Quetzi's eyes had never rested upon a creature more beautiful and seductive. He could not speak.

"Oh, great Quetzalcoatl, please, come and share a drink with me. I am honored to be in the presence of such a great god." With that, a grand oak table appeared before Quetzi. The table groaned with great bottles of pulque, large baskets of fruit, a roast pig, and many other delicacies. Quetzi's eyes focused on the pulque and he grew frightened as he remembered how he was made a fool of by the god Tezcatlipoca who disguised himself as a spider and offered Quetzi his very first taste of alcohol. But his mouth watered as he remembered the feel of booze in his mouth and the wonderful burning sensation it made as it flowed down his throat and into his belly. Quetzi shook his head and closed his eyes for a moment to clear his mind of all temptation.

"No," said Quetzi in a strong voice. "I am here to offer you a bargain."

"No," said La Diabla. "You must accept my hospitality and only then will I hear you out."

So, they sat down, Quetzi at one end of the table and La Diabla at the other. I am still a great god, he thought. I can hold my liquor. I will not fail to present my bargain. And so they ate and drank in silence, both keeping sharp eyes on each other. Finally, after an hour of this, La Diabla said, "So, what is the purpose of this visit?" As she said this, she could see that Quetzi was getting loose with the pulque. La Diabla smiled a noxious smile and waited for a response.

That poor son-of-a-bitch Quetzi! He hadn't had a drink in two months and now the pulque softened his resolve and made him think corrupt thoughts as his eyes perused La Diabla's unblemished and enticing brown skin. He shook his head again and reminded himself of his noble mission. Quetzi cleared his throat of the phlegm that pulque tends to invite from most men's throats and said, "No, I'd rather hear from you first."

La Diabla continued to smile. "Well, O magnificent Quetzalcoatl, you no doubt have heard of my plan to rid this world of the old gods. Otherwise, why would you be here?"

"Go on," he said.

La Diabla leaned forward and began, "I am sickened by the puny efforts of your hermanos and hermanas to maintain a presence in this land. They are beyond irrelevant and they do nothing more than cause a low level of nausea to permeate my very essence."

"If we are so little, why do you care?" Quetzi made a good point with this question and he rocked his head back and forth to show that he was still in command.

La Diabla leaned even closer to Quetzi and the oak table creaked. She hissed, "Because as long as the mestizos and Indians know you're still here—and they do know because of the stupid pranks you fallen gods do at night—I cannot fully rule."

Good answer, thought Quetzi. As La Diabla spoke, Quetzi allowed his eyes to drink further of her beauty. His heart beat strong within his chest and his groin flushed with the warmth of lecherous blood. What could he do? Could he forsake his fellow gods and cut a bargain to save himself and perhaps bring him a little closer to this beautiful creature? He kept still and let La Diabla continue.

"So, great Quetzalcoatl, I offer you a bargain: Do not stand in my way and, in exchange, you may have a role under my reign."

Quetzi thought for a moment. Since the conquistadors had come and banished the Aztec gods, he had lived less than a life. If he rejected La Diabla's offer and followed through with his plan to help his brothers and sisters, maybe he could rule again. And didn't he owe it to his sister after the way he had defiled her long ago? But what if he failed? This powerful dark deity of Christianity could destroy him. Maybe he could save himself and get a little power to enjoy life again! Quetzi looked into La Diabla's eyes. He could lose himself in those eyes! Screw the others! What did they ever do for him? They never visited him before this whole mess started. Screw them and his sister!

"I accept your bargain!" And he drank up another large goblet of pulque.

La Diabla laughed and walked over to Quetzi and said, "Let us walk to the outside world and start!"

So, they left the cave, arm in arm, and went to the shore on the sand and stood facing east. The smogless late summer sky gleamed a blue that no longer exists and cool wind from the ocean blew hard and clean. La Diabla touched Quetzi's sleeve and within a breath, they were standing in the Santa Ana Canyon by the northeastern desert. She lifted her hands to her mouth and screamed a mute scream and, at that very second, Quetzi saw the true power of this god. La Diabla emitted a hot and relentless wind that began as a mere breeze but then erupted into a torrent of withering heat. La Diabla blew and blew and blew for precisely three hours and Quetzi stood there without the power to move, for he was in awe.

The too-beautiful Mexicans who were once great Aztec gods could not withstand La Diabla's wind. They withered and eventually their human forms died within those three hours. Their souls rose up and went to a place beyond the moon far from their earthly home. La Diabla was now supreme!

La Diabla kept her bargain with our friend Quetzi. She let him live different lives throughout the centuries to bring his own brand of misery to the human race. First, he began as a banker, then a governor, lawyer, movie producer, editor, mass murderer, literary agent, plumber, and right now, as I speak, he is the owner of a major league baseball team. However, Quetzi never got very close to La Diabla. But his dating life was full and, so far, Quetzi has walked down the aisle at least a dozen times.

And our friend La Diabla is doing her best to strangle our world in her own way. But because of her paranoia, and despite killing all the old gods except Quetzi, she still blows the Santa Ana Winds—the devil winds, as we call them today—to make certain that the former great gods of the Aztecs will never rise again.

Is there a moral to this story? No, not really. But there is an old Mexican dicho that applies: "Si se muere el perro, se acaba la rabia." If the dog dies, the rabies will be gone. But, mis amigos, I promise you this: The dog is not dead. She is alive and well in a little town called El Pueblo de Nuestra Señora la Reina de los Ángeles de la Porciúncula.

A NEW NIGHT OF
LONG KNIVES

Brandt Jesús Cooper

When Ramón left, she got the knife out. She imagined how Ramón's
face would look cut apart. The knife was thin, long. She held the knife
in one hand, measured the blade with the span of her other hand. The
blade was three spans long. She wondered if Ramón were measuring,
whether the blade would be three spans or less.

She closed her eyes and tried in her head to see Ramón's fingers.
She could not see them. She opened her eyes. Cradled in her hands lay
the knife. Below, past the knife, jutted the open drawer. The drawer was
full of knives, all shorter than that which she held in her hands, several
of them long nonetheless. They are longer than I remembered, she
thought. At night, she thought, they lie in this drawer and grow, quietly. Soon they shall all be long knives.

She looked up from the drawer. There were words scrawled on
notes tacked to walls, cabinets, drawers. She had written some of the
notes; Ramón had written some of the others. She examined each in
turn, trying to remember by the position of the note and its shape what
was written on it. Some notes she failed to recognize. She went to these

and read them, examining the handwriting. There were four such notes. The first read, "Listen to the sound of this body dragging itself against mine." The second, "I hear the god of hands, scuttling." The third read, "Altmann: Klaus."

The last she could not read. She took it from the wall and held it in her hand. She turned it in all directions. She could not read it. She pierced the paper with the blade of the knife, pushed it down the blade to the guard, the paper slitting wider. Holding the knife before her, she walked from room to room, dampening lights.

In the darkness of the hall she sat. In her hand came the shape of the hilt and the rough, torn edge of the paper. What color was the piece of paper? In the darkness it was gray. What was written on the paper? The handwriting, she remembered, had been brittle and spiderlike, unreadable. I am a spider in the dark as well, she thought, and imagined her body becoming jointed and impossible.

Are spiders living things? She imagined her head shaved bald, stained with compounded and fragmented eyes, her fingers and toes sprouting out in slick legs, her body tightening around her womb until she was no bigger than Ramón's fist. She sat motionless, waiting without out a sound, seeing nothing but different colors of darkness.

She pressed her hand to the floor. She stood, glided slowly to the window. With the knife, she pushed the curtain open enough to see the streetlamp. She pressed her pale face to the glass.

The street outside was empty. She watched the street. The street remained empty.

She slid the latch locked on the window. She silently slid counterclockwise around the house, locking door and window. She entered the kitchen, her fingers spread before her. She touched the open drawer. She moved her hand into the drawer. She imagined the knives within cutting her hand.

She placed the long knife on the counter, just above the drawer.

She traced her way out of the kitchen, into the hall, up the stairs. She undressed her body, stretching it on a dark bed. A ray of light broke between the curtains, pale, casting an elongated triangle on her body. A knife's shape, she thought. The knives in the drawer below were growing longer. Soon, all would be long knives. Soon, the blades would push through the sides of the drawer, through the surrounding cabinets, through the walls of the kitchen, out into the streets. The white triangle of light stained her ribs. There are many things which knives are for, she thought. She moved her hand so that the light cut across the back of her wrist. Perhaps, she thought, I shall not envision anything.

She could see vague shapes but could not interpret them. She made her way down flights of stairs, through confused halls. All of a sudden, she found herself on her knees, hanging onto the edge of the knife drawer. She stood, pushed her hand into the drawer, traced the blades within. They have grown longer, she thought. She pushed the drawer shut, felt the counter above until the long knife clattered to the floor. She picked it up and took it into her hand. The note was missing from the hilt. She felt the counter for it but did not find it.

She made her way to the window. Parting the drapes, she looked out into the street. The street was empty. She slid the window open and pushed her head out, listened for the sound of footsteps.

She moved away from the window. She felt here and there, followed the walls, moved through the doors until she found herself lying on a bed. She put the knife underneath the pillow, turned the sharp edge toward the bed's head. She held her body still.

She could feel the knife beneath the pillow. She wondered if, when she woke in the morning, the knife would have burrowed its way up through the pillow to cut the back of her head and neck. She slept.

She felt things move upon her skin. Lice perhaps, or spiders. She dreamt that she was sleeping in a bed and that there were insects on her skin, but she could not open her eyes to look at them. She dreamt her way from her room down to the kitchen. She washed her eyes open with a warm rag, spreading the mucus that had sealed them down her cheeks. She looked up, saw Ramón dragging himself by his arms across the floor, toward the drawers, leaving a scarlet path behind him.

"Monarchs have scarlet paths unfurled before them. Snails leave paths behind them," she told him, "but not of blood."

"Snails," he said with fervor, "live in water or on land. Snails are shelled or unshelled."

Knives climbed over the lip of the cabinet drawer, spilled clattering to the floor.

She left Ramón to their mercy, tramping up the stairs. She could feel something on her body. She found a room with a bed in it and lay down. Beneath her head was a hard, sharp object. She touched her neck with her hand. Her hand, when she brought it away, was wet.

She could see separating her calf from her thigh a band of pale light. The light was coming through the drapes. She moved her hand into the light, saw the blood on it. She felt beneath her head for the knife, found only a scrap of paper.

She got out of bed, made her way up and down stairs, through unfamiliar halls to a kitchen. On the counter was a long knife. She went to the window. Pushing the drapes to one side, she looked out.

Outside was a pale street. It was empty. She left the window and ran her hands over her skin, brushed her hands over her skin.

She was naked. There was nothing to hide her but darkness. There was no one to hide from but herself.

She was silent. She moved step by step to the drawer. She opened the drawer and, one after one, removed the long knives.

HOTEL ARCO IRIS

Lucrecia Guerrero

DOLORES DURÁN ROLLS HER STILL-NARROW HIPS INTO AN OVER-stuffed easy chair and ignores the two sharp raps at her front door. She recognizes the knock: Mercy, her friend and washerwoman, has come to pick up the week's dirty laundry. These days it's difficult for Dolores to look at Mercy without squirming, wondering if she knows about Carlos. Well, Dolores figures, that's probably finished anyway; he hardly ever calls anymore, not even to ask what new gift she has bought him this time. And after all, what does Mercy have to worry about? She has three children and another one coming, and she's still young, at least ten years younger than Dolores. Although she doesn't look it, Dolores thinks, and pats her hair, freshly hennaed yesterday.

She listens to Mercy's heaving breathing on the other side of the door, and quietly stretches her arm in front of her, turns it to the sunlight streaming through the open space between the living room drapes. Her newest bangle sparkles, a wide circle of fourteen-karat gold, pushed midway up her forearm behind the rest of her to-the-wrist collection of gold bracelets. She's been buying one for herself every month since last year's Mother's Day. That was the seventeenth year of helping her fourth-grade students make cards of pink construction paper and red-penciled hearts for their mothers. And almost as many years of listening to some of the other teachers at Mesquite Elementary School brag in the teachers' lounge about the gifts they received from their own children at home. She spins a bracelet at her wrist. Anyway, she's better off; her lifestyle keeps her free, young. Spin, spin. Let them listen to her boast for a change.

Mercy knocks again, louder now. Doesn't she ever give up? So afraid of losing her husband, whining to Dolores, begging her to tell her if she knows anything. Dolores isn't sure if Mercy really doesn't know what's been going on or if she's just afraid to be open. With Mercy's new baby coming, she can't afford to lose the extra money that Dolores's soiled clothes bring, or the recommendations that Dolores has promised to give to the other teachers.

With the tip of her fingernail, manicured in what Perlita at the beauty salon proclaimed polish of the week, Tropicana Orange, Dolores lifts the bracelet now, slides it slowly around her arm, feels the machine-smooth coolness against her too-warm flesh. Her nails trail higher, over each bangle, onto her bare skin, higher, over feathery circles on the pale blue veins in the crook of her elbow, and drag lightly up the silkiness of her inner arm. She shivers. Her half-closed eyes don't move from the first bracelet, the outer surface of gold, etched designs of bamboo, glitter of cut edges. With painful slowness, her gaze moves to the end table at her side, the pink telephone. It is still silent, as silent as the rest of her home.

Mercy rattles the screen door and Dolores wishes she had never become friends with her in the first place. Last year Mercy's son Riquis was one of her students, so when Dolores ran into the family one night at a local park, Riquis introduced her to his parents. As she spoke with Mercy, who was apologizing for not making it to the last parent-teacher meeting and explaining that the baby had been ill, Carlos stood behind his wife. His gaze, hotter than the day's sun, melted a path down Dolores's body, paused at her breasts, lingered longer at her hips. She was shocked that he would do this with his wife standing there, even if it was out of her range of vision; still, her thoughts grew moist and warm beneath his gaze. He didn't call right away; it wasn't until later, after she and Mercy became friends, that things developed.

Mercy rattles the screen door so hard that Dolores thinks it might come off its hinges. "Isn't that you in there, Dolores?" Mercy calls.

Dolores glances up and sees Mercy's outline, eyes hand-shaded, nose pressed against the window, glass breath-steamed. "It's me, your friend Mercy."

Dolores nods, slides her hands to the edge of the armrests, presses on cabbage roses of faded scarlet, and stands up. When she opens the door, she returns Mercy's hug and says, "Sorry, I was lost in thought and didn't hear you," but pulls away when Mercy's pregnancy-swollen stomach pushes against her. Was that a tiny kick she felt?

Dolores turns and leads Mercy to the kitchen, starts a stream of words so thick and fast, Mercy can't interrupt. The coffee, Dolores says, is still hot, and she has some sweet bread that she bought yesterday across the line in Mexico, and she can't chat too long today because she has so many papers to grade because a teacher works even on Sundays, but she doesn't really mind all the work because, after all, hasn't it bought her all this? She waves her bangled arm to take in the expanse of her home.

"Yes, yes, you're very lucky," Mercy says and follows her into the kitchen. She eases her bloated body onto a kitchenette chair, the vinyl-covered seat whooshing with her weight, and groans.

"Luck has nothing to do with it, my friend," Dolores says, ignores the groan that was much too loud and prolonged to be real. "Planning and hard work, that's what it takes," she continues. "Some women choose to put their future in the hands of a man. Me? I have always taken care of myself. This is all one needs in life." She rubs her thumb against her first two fingers to signal money.

"Yes, a paycheck changes things," Mercy says. "Me, I have nothing—no job, no money." She glances at the two pillowcases full of dirty laundry propped against a kitchen cabinet. "Not that you don't pay me a fair price, no, no, I mean only that it doesn't pay enough to support me and my children. If I lose Carlitos, what will happen to me, Dolores? What will happen to me and my children?"

Dolores shakes her head slowly and stirs two teaspoonfuls of sugar into her bitter coffee. She looks away, out her kitchen window to the backyard garden: a garden of weeds, saplings from windblown seeds of unknown origins, seeds blown across the Sonoran desert to take root in her yard. She waters her garden during the yearly drought season, even though it is forbidden, fills the concrete birdbath, mushrooming out of the tangle of weeds, sits back to watch the bright rainbow that forms over the basin. She wishes there were a rainbow now.

"Ay, Dolores, you must go see this curandera," says Mercy, spews the words out so suddenly and with such force, her spit sprays across the table, an arch of saliva over the plate of bread between them.

Dolores frowns at the shift in conversation; this is not the first time Mercy has mentioned curanderas. "And why must I see a healer? I'm not sick," she says.

"I know that you're an educated woman—not ignorant like me," Mercy says. "But I tell you this one, well, she's not really a healer, she is a specialist, an adviser in matters of the heart. She can see you better than you see yourself, help you find what you are looking for." Mercy doesn't look at Dolores while she speaks; instead she studies the bread, as if choosing just the right piece were of great importance to her.

"Find love, you mean?" Dolores says, although she is not certain what she is looking for.

"Only last week I was visiting Doña Refugio, this specialist of the heart, and I mentioned you."

"Charlatans, all of them."

"Ay, mujer, I myself have used her professional services because of my little problem with Carlitos—there is no other like her."

"She probably lives too far," Dolores says.

"Not far for you. You have a car," Mercy says. "You can drive most of the way. She lives on the Mexican side—you cross the border downtown at Frontera Street, go all the way down to where the sidewalk ends, then you walk the rest of the way up the hill."

She pats her stomach and adds, "I have her, Doña Refugio, to thank for this. A packet of her powders in my man's hot chocolate every night—without telling him, naturally—and *poof.* Oh, sometimes he comes home late, like all men, but no more gone all night, you understand." She twists her wedding band, too tight on her swollen fingers.

Dolores picks at the label on a can of Carnation milk, shreds the paper into a neat pile in the center of the table. When Carlos used to crawl into her bed—sheets as cool and lonely as a desert night—he filled her head with his words of love and her body with his heat. A heat that she craves, for her blood has begun to creep cold through her veins and she feels a chill deep inside where the fever of her flesh does not reach. While she felt the sure beat of his heart next to hers, she wanted Mercy to find out, but now, well, Carlos's heartbeat has grown faint with distance and Mercy pleads silently with eyes shadowed by pain. "She didn't say for sure another woman?" Dolores says in what she hopes is a very casual tone.

"What she didn't see was the other woman's name, couldn't make out the letters." Mercy picks up the fan that's wedged between her belly and her thighs. *Swish, swish* goes the cardboard that advertises Orozco's Funeral Home *(We Respect Love of Friends and Family—Entrust Your Dead to Us, Fair Prices Guaranteed)*. "If only I knew for sure," Mercy says. "I'd pull out her hairs, the ones down there, one by one, that's what I would do."

Dolores squirm-shifts in her chair. "Now, now, my friend. Perhaps the other woman was just lonely, or maybe Carlitos misled her—sometimes men do. You know how sometimes married men complain that their wives don't behave or don't complete their duties. Maybe this woman believed him and she's lonely."

"Ha. Pretends to believe, I say. And if we can't trust our sisters, what will become of us? Look at you, you're a single woman, but you don't listen to such nonsense—oh, some gossips might say you go out with too many men, but only single men, yes?" When Dolores doesn't respond, she repeats, "Yes?"

Dolores nods. Outside a songbird perches on the rim of the crumbling birdbath, dips its tiny beak into the water, but never takes its glittering eye from Dolores. She rips the last strip of paper from the milk can. "Maybe I *will* visit this Doña Refugio, see what she has to say about my little excursion to Guaymas. Remember, I told you, I made reservations to stay at a little hotel, right there on the beach, during school break. But then I thought maybe I'll cancel. I went last year for Christmas and it wasn't so good."

"First visit this adviser," Mercy says. "See what she has to say. Who knows? Maybe this time you'll meet a special man. Not one of those tourists looking for sex, like it doesn't exist in their own house—no, no, a nice Mexican man. Someone who needs papers, maybe? Anyway, you need a rest from your students. You have not been yourself for some time now."

"Does this Doña Refugio offer you a commission for bringing her new customers?" Dolores's voice sounds more serious than she intended.

"Ay, Dolores, you always think everything is for money. No, no, it's just that she can help you discover your destiny. Anyway, you are my friend. It's not easy to find friends in this life." She rocks her weight out of the kitchen chair and says, "Well, I'd better get to my washing machine, yes?"

For a moment, Dolores doesn't move; she cannot force her eyes to meet Mercy's. In the garden, the songbird lifts its head and its throat quivers when it warbles a nameless tune that floats away on a shimmer-wave of heat. "Here, let me get that for you," Dolores says and picks up the two pillowcases of laundry. Mercy tries to link arms with her, but Dolores pulls away. "I'm sweating too much," she says.

Minutes later, in the bathroom, Dolores fills the tub, plunges her foot into the near-scalding water. Her torso sinks into the heat, water laps up onto her sides, fluid strands meeting at her waistline and lower, lacing into the mound of hair. Even there she's turning gray. How many men have there been over the years? She never wanted to be like Mercy and all the other women like her: afraid-to-be-alone women who cry over men. She worked her way through college and had no time for rela-tionships. Then as an elementary-school teacher, there were few opportunities to meet men. When she had time after grading papers and running committees, she would drop into bars, driving out of town so she wouldn't run into her students' parents, and later, former students.

Then, somewhere along the path, even before Carlos, the men began to call her only after the bars closed or to meet her in lonely alleys where their wives wouldn't see them. There, they parked their own cars and then sat back in hers while she drove them to her bed. To her bed with the sheets scrubbed free of old sex and prepared for new with a sprinkling of Chanel No. 5.

At first she had liked the relationships: no commitment. She had a need; they had a need. No complications. She was in control. But the circle of men has grown smaller, smaller, and she finds that more and more they expect gifts, even money. When did it change? What was it Carlos said to her last time, after accepting the gold-plated cigarette case and matching lighter? "Don't be so desperate, Dolores, it isn't attractive on a woman."

Even now, immersed in wet heat, she shivers at the thought of those words. But Carlos is wrong, she is not desperate. Not really. It's only that the territory has grown stale, the men of Mesquite take her for granted. She is still attractive, and thirty-nine is still young. Yes, maybe in Guaymas things can be the way they used to be.

She floats her arms on the water, slowly pushes down until the golden bracelets lie beneath the gentle waves, and thinks of treasures sinking down, down in some faraway ocean. If only she could find a new boyfriend, or if she could get a raise, she could buy . . . what? Well, something. That's all she needs to cheer her up, get things back the way they were. Her hands press, fingers spread starlike, onto her belly, push the soft flesh, the emptiness within. Tears slide off both sides of her face, over the throb of her temples, and into the still-steaming bathwater.

"How much farther?" Dolores asks.

A group of barefoot children encircles her, hungry eyes following each swing and bump of her purse. With a lace-trimmed handkerchief she dabs at the sweat on her brow. When she shades her eyes with her hand and looks in the direction of their pointed fingers, she sees the rust brown tin roofs huddled on a decline.

She nods and licks her lips to keep them from sticking together. After the children snatch the paper pesos she dangles from her finger-tips, they run away, brown skin blending into sun-baked hills. She lifts her face to catch a breeze, but it carries the stench of misery (Mercy had warned her about the nearby cesspool), so she pinches her nostrils beneath the balled-up handkerchief and presses on.

She stops in front of a shack with the door cracked and peers into the chasmlike blackness. A tip of a cigarette glows red in the darkness. Maybe this is not the answer, maybe she should turn away.

"Come in, come in," a voice calls from the interior of the shanty. Feet shuffle from the inside and the door opens wide. Doña Refugio peers up at her with eyes squinted to the sun and to the smoke from the cigarette drooping at the right side of her mouth. Her age is uncertain; too much life exposure has leathered the skin, and lines like deep cuts fan out from her eyes, which are of an unusual hazel.

Inside the one-room house, Dolores perches on the edge of the wobbly chair the adviser offers to her and listens to her own uneven breathing. Doña Refugio breaks an egg into a glass of water, studies it, cigarette bobbing between her lips. A long ash drops onto the table; she flicks it onto the plywood floor with a stained fingernail, looks up and stares into Dolores's eyes. "Hmmm," she says and nods slowly, as if what she sees reaffirms what the egg has told her.

"What's this?" she asks so suddenly that Dolores starts.

Dolores stares hard at the spot that the advisor points out, a red speck in the yolk. "Blood?"

"Of course, blood, that anyone can see." Doña Refugio flicks off another ash. "But more, a bubble of air around it, an emptiness, see? Hmmm, the soul bleeding?"

"A soul bleeding? I don't see any such thing." Dolores's tone makes it clear she doesn't like the direction this conversation is taking. She isn't in the mood for abstractions or philosophical lectures. "I want to know what the future holds," she says. "Something, someone specific."

The adviser makes smacking noises with her lips as she lights another cigarette with the butt of the one that was in her mouth. She sucks the smoke deep into her lungs before exhaling slowly through her nostrils. While she picks specks of tobacco from her lower lip, her eyes move over Dolores's face, study it as though it were a map. The hazel irises of her eyes sparkle, a sparkle that picks up Dolores's reflection, shines it back to her in a glitter of yellow lights. Her gaze drops back to the egg.

"Sí, sí," Doña Refugio mumbles to herself, then louder: "You will find your heart's desire there."

"My true love? Where? In Guaymas?" Dolores leans forward.

The adviser scoots the glass an inch closer to Dolores. "See those little ripples in the white? The ocean. Something more, hmmmm, yes, there it is, an arco iris, a rainbow." She tilts the glass toward Dolores. "Can you see yourself there?"

"Yes, yes," she says, "it's the name of the hotel, Hotel Arco Iris." Dolores stares harder but sees only an egg with a speck of blood in it. Still, she wants the empty coldness to go away. "Go on," she says, "go on."

Doña Refugio slides the egg a bit in the opposite direction. "I see a uniform, an officer, an official, or maybe a waiter. But wait, chula." She holds up her hand, the work-hardened palm creased with dark lines. "Don't put on such a face." She cackles and her hand begins to stroke her own thigh. "Hmmm, very young this new love," she says. Dolores watches the back-and-forth motion of her hand. "A man to cure that longing that wakes you up during the long nights. So long the nights, yes, querida?"

"A man who will be there all night, every night," Dolores says.

"A man of gold, one who will give you what you're looking for," the curandera says, and shuffles in broken-down men's shoes to a crate next to an army cot. She groans when she bends down to lift the crocheted doily that hangs over the side of the crate and pulls out a cigar box. She plucks out a crimson cloth and holds it up by one frayed corner. Dolores stares at it as Doña Refugio walks toward her.

"Here is the real magic," she says, gently waving the red square. "Of course, it will cost extra. I am a poor woman, after all. And you are a person who never underestimates the value of money. Everything has its price—that's what you say, yes?"

"Is it silk?" Dolores says and slides it between her thumb and index finger.

"Almost, almost." Doña Refugio tugs it away from Dolores's grasp.

Dolores pulls bills from her wallet and lays them on the table one by one until the adviser finally nods in agreement.

She pats the sweat from Dolores's face with the scarf, tucks it into the breast pocket of the other woman's blouse, plucks at it so a corner droops out. "Earlier, I treated it with a strong potion of love. Wear it over your heart. It will reveal to all the truth that lies inside."

Two weeks later, after unpacking in Room 19 of the Hotel Arco Iris, Dolores, her high heels a hollow echo on the ceramic tiles, follows the headwaiter through the hotel's dining room. He wears a uniform of bolero jacket and black slacks, but she can tell by the studied sway of his round hips that this one is not for her. He hesitates at a booth, but she shakes her head. "No, there," she says and points to the center of the cavernlike room.

Once her eyes become accustomed to the shadows, she sees many of the regulars she met during last year's Christmas break, now sprinkled around the dark room, each alone at a candlelit table. She shared cocktails with most of them last year, these pilgrims to the Hotel Arco Iris, but something about them—she can't say what—frightens her.

She nods to Bill, a Korean War vet, his wheelchair angle-parked by the wall to keep the passage clear. Last year he had his sleepy attendant push him to Dolores's room at four in the morning, where he cried whiskey tears. He pulled out a tattered lonely-hearts magazine and turned it to the ad he had placed:

FINANCIALLY SECURE American seeks traditional young Mexican girl for marriage. Must send photograph with first letter. Will pay passage for first meeting with the right gal.

After speaking with him, Dolores discovered that his teenage pen pal had arrived to a meeting expecting to see a tall, young soldier, the man that Bill was before losing the bottom half of his legs in Korea so many years ago. Dolores wonders if this year Bill will meet a girl poor enough to pretend to see him as he wants to be seen.

Her fingertips graze the scarf that she tied into a bow around the spaghetti straps of her sundress and lets her gaze roam again. Now it rests on the too-thin businesswoman from Tucson, on her intelligent face that collapses in disillusioned folds. During the last visit, her room, two doors down from Dolores's, faced the seashore, and in the evening, the woman, naked from her bath, lay on her bed in the glow of a scarf-covered lamp. And every evening, Dolores peeked through the slats of her own shutters and saw a beach boy's lithe silhouette break away from the moon shadows, slide over the windowsill and slip into the other woman's room. The young man always left in the still magical moments before the dawn, no doubt with a little something for his time, stuffed inside his swimming trunks.

And over there in the farthest corner sits the history professor from Mexico City, his soft body heaped onto a chair like a melting mound of ice cream. That one never volunteers to join the other pilgrims for a nightcap; he tries to avoid them. But Dolores has heard the maids talking and knows that the professor is married and from a respectable family, but comes here to negotiate deals that will soothe the needs that throb through his gnarled veins. Already there is a bruise beneath one eye. It is said that those injuries cost him many extra pesos. How does he explain those souvenirs to his family year after year? Now she can almost feel him shiver with anticipated pain when a muscular young waiter arrives to take his order.

She stares blankly at the end of the room, French doors opened to the terraza. Her thoughts travel outside to the night, to steps leading to the beach and the lap of ocean waves beyond. Her body fills with a great sadness.

"Would you like another drink, Señora?" A waiter bends over her, so close that his lips tickle the outer rim of her ear.

She jerks away, and he touches her forearm as if to calm her. The hairs on her arm spring up like sentinels. She takes this as a sign: He is the one. Dolores twists her body around so that he can see the scarlet cloth tied in a bow over her heart. He is very young. "Señorita," she corrects him, then adds, "You aren't the same waiter, the one who brought my drinks. I would have remembered you."

"I was already leaving for the day, but I just happened to see you and, pues, something, who can say what, pulled me straight to you, Señorita." His words are singsong like those of a child who has memorized a poem that means more to someone else than to him.

She looks sharply at him, but his face remains smooth and impassive. His finger plays with the edge of her bow, then he cups it in his hand, and a bit of red, like a drop of blood, peeps out between his fingers.

"So pretty," he says, and his lips stretch back over his teeth, more to one side than the other; a smile practiced in the mirror.

When she compliments him on his gold tooth, she hears her own voice and thinks that it trembles as much as her heart.

"Please permit me to join you," he says and pulls out a chair, waits for her answer.

Dolores looks away. The others in the room are watching, the flame from the candle on each table throwing a shadow on each face.

"I would like to order a bottle of Chivas," he says, "but I'm a little low on cash at the moment." He hesitates, adds, "Maybe some other time." Still standing, he scoots the chair back slightly.

Dolores presses her hand over her eyes and indicates the candle with her chin. "My eyes," she says. "They're delicate, you understand."

He smiles, leans forward, and spits on the tiny flame. It dies with a barely perceptible hiss.

EL BRONCO Y
LA LECHUZA

René Saldaña, Jr.

EL BRONCO, THE BUCKING BRONC, STUMBLED OUT OF THE CANTINA, still cursing the other patrons. Throughout the evening, he had drunk tequila, picked fights with every man in the bar smaller than he, and bullied the littlest of the men, Mr. Jacinto, the local scribe and poet, to give up his half bottle of tequila. "I need it for the road back home," he'd screamed to the tiny man wearing a vest and thick glasses.

"But it is my bottle, Señor Miguel. I have worked hard all week. The doctor tells me one glass a week will help me with my digestive problems." Mr. Jacinto was the only man allowed to bring his own bottle into the bar because of his ailments. The town doctor, Doctor Martínez, had told Ramiro the bartender, "Sí, he needs his one drink per week. I bought him a bottle from your bar, compadre, and he loves to sit and listen to the other men talk. He says he gets ideas for his poems sometimes. So, por favorcito, compadre, if you would let him bring in the bottle for his one drink, I'd be indebted to you always." Truth was, Ramiro the bartender was indebted to Doctor Martínez for having come in the middle of the night to help deliver his three daughters. Ramiro the bartender

151

had okayed the bottle and passed on the word that Mr. Jacinto's bottle was off limits to any of the others. "Es su medicina," he told the men. "It is his medicine." He somehow felt greater for having said that. As though he himself were a doctor prescribing the cure.

"Señor Miguel," said Mr. Jacinto, who never called the drunken man Bronco for fear of a fist in his mouth, "I have had that bottle for over two months. How can you take it from me just like that? If you want, you can have a glass of it as a gift, but to take the entire bottle is ludicrous."

"Lady Cruz? Who is this Lady Cruz?" slurred the drunkard.

"Tu madre, your mother," whispered one of the men from behind his glass of beer.

"Who said that?" charged Bronco, bottle in hand, choked at the neck. "Be a man! Say it to my face!"

No one dared, though.

"I didn't think so. In this town, yo soy el único hombre!"

"And because you are the only real man in town, Señor Miguel," tried to reason Mr. Jacinto, "I know you will be fair and return my bottle."

"Ha, ha, ha, haaa! I didn't say I was a reasonable man, amigo, all I said was that I was the only man, so I will not return your bottle." He stumbled out of the bar then, whinnying some nonsense about how all the men in the bar were cobardes, spineless cowards, because they would say bad things about him or his mother only to his back, but never, "NEVER! Never to my face."

He began the mile walk back to his house in the monte. The woods, as on every other night, were unnaturally dark. "Mr. Jacinto has traveled many places," Ramiro the bartender was fond of saying, "and he has never found a place darker than the montes of Cuernos Rojos at night." El Bronco ignored tonight's darkness as he did every other night, taking for granted its beauty, its wondrous majesty.

"Hijos de la chi . . . ," he started when he heard the men behind him laughing, still in the bar, then he stopped speaking when he heard a terrible fluttering above his head. He looked up to the sky, but the clouds were too heavy for the stars to show themselves. He heard the noise again, and this time he shuddered at feeling a blowing on his bare neck. El Bronco turned to go back to the bar to get some help, but thought better of it. "Esos good for nothings," he mumbled. "Whatever it is, it's gone now, anyway."

He continued walking down the worn path toward his house, some three quarters of a mile farther still. I'll be okay, he thought, because soon I will be reaching "los dos amantes"—two mesquites that grew on opposite sides of the path, sprawling out and hanging over it. It was called "the two lovers" because the branches had somehow grown and braided themselves one with another to form an embrace. The younger lovers, though, called it "el árbol de la buena suerte" because the branches looked like crossed fingers. Here had been the place for young men to meet the young women to whom they would propose, and there had been more acceptances than rejections under the trees' shadows, thus, aptly dubbed "the tree of good luck."

As he was approaching the "lovers" or the "luck," he became aware that there, on the elbows of the branches, was perched a lechuza, a giant white owl. He stopped cold. El Bronco remembered the stories his grandmother had told him about owls. They are witches, shapeshifters, who come out at night in this form in the hopes of exacting revenge on those who have done them wrong. He remembered she said that no one should curse at an owl ever because it would swoop down on the dirty-mouthed child and pluck his eyes out from their sockets and rip him limb from limb.

The man laughed. "Esa viejita loca," he shouted at the bird.

"Hoo!" the bird screeched. "Hoo!"

El Bronco reared, it seemed. He was ready to hightail it back to the cantina. He heard a roar of laughter wafting from the bar. He decided he would not go back. After all, he thought, this is only an owl, and my grandmother's stories were only stories, and I am a man afraid of nothing, not even the devil himself. He began cursing at the lechuza, listing in alphabetical order every bad word he had ever learned. He even invented a few that were curse words only because he muttered them in anger.

"Hoo! Who have you done wrong to tonight?" asked the owl.

El Bronco felt a warm stream of urine trickling down his leg. He made the sign of the cross using both index fingers as his grandmother had taught him, and as he'd seen Dracula's victims do in that film the good doctor showed in his backyard on a white sheet. "This act," his grandmother had warned, "this connection to God, will save you from the lechuza's evil intent. It will know God is with you and fly away."

Tonight, though, it wasn't working. This owl, this bruja, was not going to be deterred from its obvious goal. Leaving a trail of urine on the dusty path under him, Bronco turned tail and ran as hard and as fast as he ever had. His knees bumped against his elbows. "Arghhh!" he screamed. "¡Ayúdenme! Help me! She's after me! She's going to kill me!"

Back at the cantina, the dejected little poet with the thick glasses heard these distant ravings and suddenly asked the men at the bar, "Did you hear that?" They turned to him, mildly interested. "It sounds like a madman coming from the montes."

Normally the others would ridicule a man making such a statement because in their inebriated states they knew—some had even experienced for themselves—that the sound of the wind could transform itself into the voice of a beautiful woman beckoning or the moans of a dying grandfather. Once, it had even transformed itself into the cries for help from a Japanese soldier. That one the bar's regulars did not let go of easily. They laughed at Don Macario for weeks when he admitted rather loudly in the bar that he had heard a Japanese soldier asking, wailing for help. He had served in the Second World War and occasionally suffered from flashbacks. The others could not sympathize with his not going to fight the enemy.

But now they didn't laugh. They knew Mr. Jacinto had not had even his one shot of tequila for the week and had refused offers from all the patrons. So what he heard must have been for real. "There it is again. It sounds . . . ," began one man.

"It sounds like El Bronco screaming like a little girl," said Ramiro the bartender. The men did not laugh, though. Even though the man had left the bar, they were still afraid of him. They couldn't even look at Ramiro the bartender when he spoke those words. Because if I make eye contact, they thought, it means I agree with him, and if Bronco finds out, then it's the end of me.

"Let's go outside to see what's happening," offered up the most drunk of the men.

"Yes," agreed the others, "let's go."

The last of them had filled in the spot beside Mr. Jacinto, who was standing in the middle of them all, to form a half circle. They strained their eyes into the darkness that oozed from the woods, but saw nothing. They turned their ears slightly in that direction, and there it was again. They were certain. It was El Bronco, and most of them thought, He is screaming like an eight-year-old girl.

Then a shadow began to take form, growing darker and closer and louder. "Help me! She's going to kill me!" He was now out of the woods and running at full gallop toward the men. He didn't even look over his shoulder when he came to a halt and fell to his knees before Mr. Jacinto. He placed the bottle at his side, clasped his hands as if in prayer, and begged Jacinto and the others to protect him, at which point the men in the semicircle pinched their noses shut with their fingers because not only had the big bucking bronco of a man peed in his pants, but he'd gone and done number two, as well.

Mr. Jacinto put his hand on the man's shoulder and said, "What is it, Señor Miguel? What is chasing you?"

"Por favorcito, Mr. Jacinto, please, please, please, save me from her!"

"Who? Who's chasing you?" he asked.

Bronco couldn't believe his ears. Had Jacinto said "who" or "hoo"?

The smaller man smiled down at the kneeling man, his hands still clasped. It can't be, he thought. My drunken mind is playing horrible tricks on me. "La Lechuza," he rasped.

The other men stepped back, for they knew the stories also. Their parents and grandparents had been witness or had fallen victim to the Great White Owl with magical powers. They all sucked in a breath as though it could be their last and looked into the darkness. And sure enough, almost at the edge of the monte, they saw a white object flying toward them. They stepped back once more. But Jacinto didn't. He held his ground, looking up at the quickly approaching white figure.

"Yo me voy," said one of the men, who turned to walk into the bar.

"I'm with you," followed another.

The rest stayed behind, literally scared stiff. They couldn't move anymore.

As the figure flew closer, one of the men began to whisper a laugh. The others turned to him, shocked that he would dare laugh at Bronco, then back at the figure, and they, too, began to laugh. Loudly now. Jacinto smiled; Bronco slowly, very carefully and full of fear, turned also.

"It's nothing more than a white-winged dove, Bronquito," said one of the men, still hidden behind the crowd of other men. "Es una palomita blanca, mansito." Now they were all laughing hard and calling the man little bronco, a pony, and tame.

The kneeling man looked back at Mr. Jacinto, who was still smiling at him, and said, "Mr. Jacinto, here is your bottle. And I am so very sorry for the wrong I have done to you."

"That's okay, my friend. No problem. Would you like to join me for that glass I offered earlier?" he said, helping the big man up. "Una copita to calm your nerves?"

"No, gracias, Mr. Jacinto. In light of the circumstances," said Bronco, pointing with his eyes to his messed pants, "I must go home and clean myself up. But thanks again, sir." Up on his feet, he hesitantly turned to the woods and slowly inched his way back to the edge, walking very calmly, until he thought the others could not see him anymore, and then he began to run at full speed, never slowing to look back or around until he had reached his house safely.

MICHELLE'S MIRACLE

Kelley Jácquez

ONE SUNDAY THE PRIEST AT OUR LADY OF THE VIRGEN DE GUADALUPE ascended to the pulpit with the help of his altar boys and then hung onto the lectern with both hands while he attempted to recite the opening liturgy. His words were slurred, and his body kept waving about as if struggling to stand straight against the roll of a ship. Finally Father Morris gave up his charade, leaned full against the pulpit, curling his hands over the front edge, and smiled.

"There was a man," began Father Morris. The old priest rubbed at the hair above his right temple, making the white tufts stand out like miniature snow flurries and sending his biretta to sit precariously akimbo on one side of his head.

"And a flood comes. So this man crawls up on top of his house, tú sabes, to get away from the flood. And he starts praying. He believes he is a good Christian and a powerful believer in the miracles of God."

At this point Father Morris began to laugh as if the story were over, but soon he resumed his narrative while the congregation sat mesmerized by the scene before them.

"So this man thinks he's really a very good Christian, and he's praying, and he thinks if he prays hard enough God will send a miracle to save him from the rising water. Entonces, this other man comes by in a rowboat and tells him to jump in. But the man on top of the house says, 'Gracias amigo, pero I know that God is going to send me a miracle.' So the man in the rowboat paddles off and the man on the roof begins to pray again.

"Y muy pronto, a helicopter comes by and a rope ladder is thrown to the man on the roof. But the man waves the helicopter away and begins to pray otra vez.

"Then, the next thing he knows, a huge wave of water washes over the roof of his house and the man is swept away and drowns. The man's soul ascends to heaven and when he arrives, God comes to greet him. But the man, he looks very confused, so God says to him, 'What is it, my son?' And the man says, 'I believed in you all my life; I believed you would save me. But you let me drown. Why?'

"God looked at the man and answered, 'I sent you a boat and a helicopter, what more did you want?' "

Father Morris looked out at his parishioners as if expecting them to join him in laughter and comprehension, and was met only with rows of blank eyes. The priest blinked several times behind his thick glasses, stretched his corrugated neck like a turtle inspecting its environment, then turned away and flapped an arm at the congregation as he descended the steps, mumbling. "Go look for boats and helicopters," said Father Morris, "they are all around you." And with that he left the congregation sitting as still as stone and went back to bed.

⸙┼⸝═⸜┼⸙

It was the winter of 1979 and northwest New Mexico had been warned to brace itself for one of the coldest winters on record. The newsmen had forecast it, and even more convincing, the Navajo medicine men had predicted it long before the official report. The medicine men had watched the little creatures hoarding food earlier than they usually do, and hoarding more of it. They watched the hair of horses grow thicker before the first freeze had ever happened. They had been watching these things for centuries and were never wrong.

It was unfortunate that on a night when the temperature would reach no higher than three degrees, Freddie Fender was to sing at McGee Park. McGee Park is the closest thing to a concert hall near Farmington. It's where they hold the wrestling matches, the classic car displays, the horse shows, and the rodeos. For the Freddie Fender show the sawdust and horse manure had been swept up, folding chairs had been set out, and colored lights had been hung.

Salina Gonzales checked her purse for the tickets to the concert and left her husband at home as she always did, because he didn't like going anywhere anyway, and drove to the house of Marina Sánchez. Salina was a woman who accepted life for just what it was, neither railing against it nor speaking in favor of it. Nothing seemed to bring Salina to her knees. Not her taciturn husband, not the daughter who ran away and then called home intermittently to scream garbled obscenities over the phone, and not the son who had been accused of molesting the daughter of the woman he was living with in North Carolina and had hanged himself before the trial. At the funeral of her son, Salina shocked those who sat closest trying to comfort her when she said that it was better to be the mother of a son who committed suicide than the mother of a convicted child molester, and she was grateful to her son for making the choice.

When Marina got into the car, she asked Salina if she had had any trouble getting away from her husband, and Salina answered no, there was no trouble. He just hid behind his copy of the farm news the way he always did, all sour at the mouth, and grunted when she reached for the handle of the front door. Marina had laughed and said, "Oh, come on, Salina, you know he smiles once a year whether he needs to or not." Salina told Marina not to take his annual smiles too seriously. "It's probably because he's just run over something small and helpless with the tractor," said Salina.

Marina was a widow with grown children who now spent most of her time knitting doilies and afghans to put into Matty's Gift Shop in Bloomfield. She missed her husband and missed being married. She went to wedding dances and funerals and to Grandparents Without Partners gatherings in Albuquerque once a month looking for another husband. But, although she didn't know it, she was really looking for her dead husband and would never marry again. This night the two women, dressed in the frocks they usually wore to weddings, had planned to leave all they had known in the past and become two young girls again while watching a Mexicano idol who conjured heart flutters like those of the first time they had ever been alone with a boy. Filled with youth, the women giggled as they passed the El Nido Bar, then turned around and pulled into the parking lot vowing just one drink and only one song on the jukebox.

Della Mondregal was already at the bar, although why she had picked what was to be one of the coldest nights in El Nido's recorded history to get tired of drinking alone was anybody's guess. It was rumored that Della was dying of cancer. Nobody knew what kind or if she was doing anything about it. They just knew that she stayed in her home most of the time, had the phone disconnected, and quit coming to mass at Our Lady of Guadalupe.

Della was the only child of one of El Nido's few mixed marriages in 1921 between a Spanish woman and an Anglo man. This did not cause Della any problems, however, because the townspeople knew that her father was often the reason they had meat throughout the winter. So if anything, Della was treated with special respect by the children she played with. Her life took a drastic change for the worse when her father rode away for the last time. Her mother never got over it. She remembered watching her mother sit at the top of the road with her arm raised against the brilliant glitter of the evening sun until she no longer needed to shield her eyes from the glare and walked back into the house with slumped shoulders and sagging eyes. Sometimes Della sat with her mother watching the road, but more often she played by herself or cooked something for her mother to eat when the day's vigil was over. Della had not minded that she had been born to a mother who had been rendered deaf and mute by scarlet fever until after her father went away, for it was then that her mother really quit talking. It was then that Della came to know that silence wails; it thunders through a house and is kept there until the wood inside the walls vibrates with its misery.

While still a child, Della decided that she would grow up and have many children and that her house would be filled with many people all talking at once, so she married Alejandro Mondregal when she was seventeen and prayed to get pregnant on her wedding night.

She did not get pregnant on her wedding night or any other night throughout her marriage, and by the time her husband died they had not spoken to each other, except to say "pass the salt" or something of the kind, for fifteen years. Only later, much later, did Della realize that some people receive the legacy they are going to inherit for the rest of their lives, at birth.

Della had been at the bar for about an hour when Hortencia Alcón hobbled into the bar and used her cane to shut the door. Hortencia said it was too late and too far to drive to the feed store in Bloomfield for teat medicine, so she was coming to get some strong whiskey to rub on the cow's udder before treating it with Corona Bag Balm. Della looked at her through half-closed eyes, saying she was impressed as hell with Hortencia's home remedies and told Ruby the bartender to bring Hortencia whatever she was drinking. The old woman wasn't prone to drink, and she really had come to the bar in search of relief for her cow and not herself, but she knew Della was dying and thought it would cost her nothing to fill the space next to Della for just a little while.

After parking her car about 100 yards up the road leading behind the bar, Dolores Álvarez was at the bar waiting for her husband to come in. No one was quite sure what was to happen after Geraldo Álvarez entered the bar, but whatever it was, the people of El Nido had grown to rely on the Álvarezes to have a fight once every two or three months, and looked forward to a new story concerning the latest scrimmage. The reason for a fight might be as simple as an infidelity, or as contrived and complicated as the need for dramatic displays of affection.

Everyone's favorite story was about the time Dolores bought a gun and drove to the Montoya Pick-a-Dent wrecking yard, resolved to murder Geraldo after finding a tube of lipstick—not her color—on the floorboard of the car. She had cried the whole way, making her face swollen and red, and when she drove past the wrecking yard office, Freddie Montoya grabbed his keys, locked up the greasy office, and left for the day. He had seen that face before on a couple of ex-wives and decided it was best to let love take its natural course without any witnesses or innocent bystanders.

Dolores wound her car along the narrow path leading deeper into the piles of twisted metal until she came to a broad spot in the road and pulled over. She checked her lipstick in the rearview mirror and began loading bullets into the pistol as the man at the pawn show had shown her. When she finished, she noticed she hadn't removed the price tag hanging from the trigger guard and then was afraid to take it off now that the gun was loaded. She left it where it was, hoping it wouldn't get in the way.

She walked up the road, calling Geraldo's name until he appeared from behind a rusted Plymouth. He smiled at Dolores, dropping his wrench in the dirt as he walked toward her with his hands turned out, but his smile grew dull and fell into slackened lips of disbelief as Dolores raised the gun. It looked like a toy with its tiny mechanisms, pea-sized barrel, and stupidly swinging price tag, but Geraldo knew the gun was no toy and Dolores's face told him this was no joke. Geraldo did what he felt any real man would do at a time like this and took off running for all he was worth.

He heard the first pop and then a ricochet as the bullet bounced off a decapitated Ford. The second bullet whizzed past his face and the third spun off into thin air. Another ended up hitting the dirt at about the same time as Geraldo did, his feet tangled in distributor wires and sagebrush. Dolores walked toward him, pointing the gun at his chest. She had to think for a second which side his heart was on, then remembered the pledge of allegiance and aimed to the left. Dolores pulled the trigger, then pulled it again and Geraldo screamed like a woman in childbirth. Dolores kept pulling the trigger and Geraldo kept screaming until finally Dolores threw the gun down on the ground and plunked herself next to Geraldo in the dirt.

"Goddammit, Dolores, you could have killed me!"

"But the gun quit working, Geraldo. Why do you think it did that?" Dolores picked up the gun and began inspecting it as if she might know what to look for.

"Well now, goddammit, Dolores, it probably jammed." Geraldo smoothed back his hair with both hands. "Where'd you buy it?"

"At the Honest Deal Pawn Shop in Bloomfield. Paid forty-five dollars for it."

"Well now, there ya go. A gun like that, a working gun, shoulda cost ya three times that. Pawnshops are like mechanics, honey. Women shouldn't deal with them unless they got a man standing there with 'em. You can't be too careful, baby. Some people just ain't honest." With that, Geraldo put his arm around Dolores and the two of them drove home and lived happily ever after for a good three months until Geraldo staggered through the door one night with his beard smelling of perfume.

Dolores had pretty much given up on guns the night she sat at the El Nido Bar waiting for her husband to come through the door, so everyone figured that the gun in the junkyard story would remain the reigning favorite. Still, they were happy to stick around for whatever happened.

While Salina and Marina drove toward the bar, Beany Moreno was walking toward it from her home across El Nido Highway. She was not looking for customers this night; the season for deer hunters and fishermen was over and they had all gone back to wherever they lived the rest of the year. Mainly she was bored and wanted to talk to someone besides her small daughter or aged parents. Beany was El Nido's only paid prostitute. Nobody really minded that Beany was a prostitute because her work was seasonal and she didn't believe in stepping out to a car with the husband of someone she knew. This sort of selective morality made it easy for the women of El Nido to accept her, ignore her profession, and keep her as one of their own.

Beany stepped up to the door as Salina pulled her car into the parking lot and honked a hello. Beany waited for the women to climb out of the car and all three of them entered El Nido Bar laughing at Salina's joke about a man who finds a magic bottle and a genie who grants him one wish. The man wishes to be twice as smart as he already is, so the

genie turns him into a woman. The three women joined Della and
Hortencia and Dolores at the bar and they all gushed at what a coincidence it was to see each other there since it was seldom that they were
in the same place at the same time unless it was at church for a funeral. Dolores asked what the women had been laughing at as they entered
the bar and Salina told the joke again. The women whooped and
squealed until Ruby the bartender teased that they would crack glass-
ware if they kept it up.

After ordering a round for everyone, including Adolfo Flores and
Luis Viegas, who sat at the other end of the bar feeling invaded, Salina
went to the jukebox and punched the numbers for Freddie Fender.
"We're on our way to see him tonight," smiled Salina. All of the women
were impressed and all except Della offered reasons why they hadn't
bought tickets themselves.

"I forgot all about it," said Beany.

"I knew I would have to work," said Ruby, setting down the glasses Salina had ordered.

"I knew my husband wouldn't take me and he would be mad if I
went without him," said Dolores.

"Who is Freddie Fender?" asked Hortencia. No one heard her, so no
one answered, and they went on to swoon to the song on the jukebox.

"Do you think there are really any men who love their women like
the words in the song?" said Dolores. "Hell no," said Salina. "They just
make that shit up so we'll marry them and clean up after them."

"Well," said Dolores, "maybe they'd appreciate us more if they were
the ones to have the babies. Maybe then things would be different."
Beany said no, that wouldn't work because they would just whine about
the pain and the women would have to take care of them even more.
"You know what it's like when they have the flu or get a cut on a finger. No, I'll have the babies just so I don't have to listen to them
complain." The women agreed; yes, in the end it was easier just to have
the babies themselves.

Adolfo and Luis motioned for Ruby and shoved the money for a six-
pack across the bar and left. As the men closed the door behind them the
women teased them that they couldn't take their own medicine.

Marina ordered another round and when everyone had a glass she lifted her drink and said, "Here's to birth control. If they'da had it when I was in high school I'da had me a ball." The women clinked their glasses and Hortencia said, "From what I hear, you had a ball anyway. It was only by some miracle you didn't get pregnant." Marina scrunched her face at Hortencia but laughed right along with the rest of the women.

"You know what's really a miracle, though," said Dolores softly. "It's really the babies themselves, que no? When I had my first child I really thought I was the first woman to do that." Oh yes, the women agreed. "Actually, my first baby really was a miracle because they said she wasn't going to live. They said she had something wrong with her heart. So I prayed and prayed, y mira, my Sophia will graduate next June. I think God cured her."

"Ah," belched Della, "the doctors just didn't know what they were saying. She probably wasn't sick at all to begin with."

"No, she was!" shrilled Dolores.

"Is OK, don't listen to her," Hortencia patted Dolores's hand, "she's just being hard to get along with esta noche. I believe in miracles. I have always believed that one happened to me once." All of the women except Della, who rolled her eyes, encouraged Hortencia to tell about the miracle.

"When I was a little girl, I guess about five years old because my father had just died," Hortencia said, looking up at the ceiling as if the facts written in her memory would be printed there. "Yes it was then. I found my mother sitting out in front of the house crying. I thought she was crying because she had just lost my father, but that wasn't it at all, come to find out years later. She was crying because there wasn't anything to eat in the house. I remember we'd had sweet corn and tortillas for breakfast that morning. What I did not know was my mother had fed me and my four brothers and sisters the last of the food without eating anything herself."

The women sat quietly listening to Hortencia's story, each of them recalling a time when there was only tortillas and a little of something else set on the table to eat.

"I guess she didn't know what to do," continued Hortencia, "so she called all of us together and said we should go for a walk. I think she was hoping there might be some asparagus still growing along the ditch bank, or at least some mint leaves for tea." Wetting her lips, Hortencia added, "I still like mint tea."

"We took our walk and returned with some skinny asparagus shoots and some bug-eaten mint leaves, and left them on the kitchen table. My mother was so tired she lay across the bed and fell asleep. Hours later, mis hermanos and me went in to wake her up, crying that we were hungry. She sat on the side of the bed and told us that we would have to fill our stomachs with the tea that night. But we all began talking at once, all of us trying to tell her that there was plenty of food. She shook her head but allowed us to drag her to the kitchen anyway where we told her to look inside the cold box. My brother, unable to wait for her to pull the handle, opened it for her and I watched as my mother's eyes grew to the size of plates. 'How could this be?' I remember she whispered. There, inside the cold box were two whole chickens, potatoes, and green beans wrapped in brown paper, and three quart jars of milk. Under the table sat a sack of flour and a bucket of dried pinto beans." Hortencia stared down at the top of the bar with tears clinging to her sparse gray lashes. " 'It is all the food in the world!' my mother whispered."

All of the women sat very still for a moment or two. Then Della said, "It was probably just a neighbor though, someone who knew your mother needed help." Hortencia looked up at Della and opened her mouth to speak but Beany did it for her. "That's kind of a miracle too though, isn't it? I mean, that they knew she needed help. And then wanted no thanks."

The women outvoted the shake of Della's head, agreeing that it qualified as a miracle. Then Dolores said that now that she thought about it, she was sure she'd had a miracle too. "I'd forgotten all about this. That's funny," mused Dolores, "I told myself I'd never forget about this."

"Tell us, tell us!" chimed the women.

"I was driving back from Gallop. I was so tired and yet I was too afraid to pull over. It was night, and you know how deserted it is along that road. I was afraid that if someone found me asleep in the car they might, you know, do God knows what and no one would have seen a thing. There's nothing out there, you know, nothing at all along that one stretch. So I kept driving. I didn't realize I'd fallen asleep at the wheel until I felt the hand."

Dolores put her own hand down to a place just above her knee. "A strong hand had taken hold of my leg and shaken it so hard that I could still feel the hand on my thigh after I'd come awake and swerved away from almost hitting a culvert." She shook her own leg. "I felt a hand," said Dolores with finality.

"I can feel it now," she said dreamily and rubbed the place on her leg where she said she felt the hand.

Della had been fishing in her empty glass for a piece of ice, and without looking up, said, "Sí, tonta, tú tienes una hand on your leg. It is your own."

She popped the piece of ice into her mouth as if she had delivered the last word on the subject.

"Goddammit, Della . . ." began Dolores.

"Escuche, you pro'bly just hit a bump and your leg hit the shifting stick. Or your purse fell against your leg." Little bursts of water from the crunching ice flew from Della's mouth and landed on the bar as she spoke.

"The car was an automatic," said Dolores through clenched teeth. "And I know what I felt, Della. I felt a hand shaking my leg just like I'm going to shake your face if you don't stop talking all sour grapes." Della went back to digging in her glass for ice cubes with a curve at her lips like that of a mother who'd just listened to a fish tale from a child.

"I've got one too," said Beany. "I mean, I think it's a miracle."

Just at that moment the door to the bar opened and in danced Michelle De la Cruz, shivering and rubbing her hands. The women greeted her and wondered out loud what had brought her to the El Nido Bar on such a cold night when they had never seen her there before even in good weather. Michelle looked around the bar and see-ing only women, asked if that night had been designated as an official hen party night at the El Nido Bar. "Oh, I get it," she said, "the men's bodies are stashed in the back, verdad?" The women laughed and told her to sit down.

"No puedo, Señoras, I must return to my children. I have come only to buy some sodas. I promised them sodas, then forgot them when I was in town. I haven't had peace since I showed up without them."

The women told her that they were discussing miracles and that Beany was just about to tell them about her own.

"Well, perhaps I can stay for just one miracle," smiled Michelle. She leaned against a stool next to Dolores, near the door.

"I don't *really* know if it was a miracle," said Beany, suddenly shy, "but it kind of feels like one because my little girl is still alive."

The women leaned closer to Beany and encouraged her to go on.

"Well, it was so strange. You know how the television never works out here?" They all nodded and agreed that the reception was unpredictable at best.

"This one day," continued Beany, "I had turned it on to see if I could get anything on the damned thing. I was going to do my ironing. Anyway, I was even willing to settle for the news, and that's what was on. There was this man showing this hemlock—no the hemler—no—¿cómo se llama? What is it where you save someone from choking to death by grabbing them around the middle from behind?"

"I know, I know!" called out Salina, bouncing on her bar stool. But before she could say the words Della answered, "the Heimlich maneuver." Salina glared at Della but Della paid no attention, so Salina put her elbow back on the bar, resting her chin in her hand, and continued to listen to Beany's miracle.

"Yes, that's it," said Beany, "the him lack."

"So this man came on and he showed how you grab a person, and if you do it just right, the thing that's choking them flies out of their mouth. He said you can tell if someone is really choking because they can't make any sound. They can't cough, or wheeze, or nothing. He said if the person can make any kind of sound they're probably going to be all right."

The women nodded that they understood that no air meant no sound.

"I watched the man, and wouldn't you know, as soon as he finished showing the hemlock manure the television went snowy again."

Beany paused, taking a sip from her glass.

"Well," said Della, with a scowl, "there might be a miracle in there somewhere if you learned how to pronounce "Heimlich.""

The women looked daggers at Della while Beany went on with the story.

"No, no, that's not the end. Later that day I was ironing and my little girl came saying she was hungry, so I gave her an orange. I had peeled it and pulled it into sections and she sat down at the table to eat it. I could see her from where I stood at the ironing board, but mostly I wasn't looking up, but just ironing away, thinking of nothing, you know how you do."

All of the women nodded, affirming that they knew exactly the sorts of things women think of when they iron.

"Then it hit me," said Beany. "I didn't hear anything. I looked up and my little girl was sitting so still. I mean, I never realized before that day how much noise a person makes just by breathing, just by being alive. And when the noise is gone, it's *soooo* silent."

The women bent even closer to Beany.

"I remember thinking as I walked to my daughter, Ay Dios, I hope this works. I hope that man knew what he was talking about. Her mouth was open but nothing could come out. So I grabbed her from the chair and put my arms around her from behind."

"Where? Where did you put your arms?" asked Dolores.

"Right here," said Beany, and showed everyone where they should put their arms to save the life of a person who is choking.

"Then you pull back, kinda quick, kind of snapping the knot you've made with your hands right there in front, and that makes the extra air force out whatever got caught."

The women were in awe of Beany's expertise.

"I don't know what I would have done if I hadn't seen that man on television," said Beany, shaking her head at the very thought.

The women stared at Beany and shook their heads with the same slow terror of being unprepared to save a child's life.

"Do you think it was a miracle?" asked Beany. "Would that be considered a miracle?"

"Well," huffed Hortencia, "it's every bit a miracle as finding food in the cold box."

"Yes, I think that's a miracle," said Dolores with her eyebrows knitted together.

"No doubt about it," confirmed Salina. "I mean, the television came on just long enough for you to see that man, and then it was gone."

The women were nodding at each other and all speaking at once. Each of them was smiling at Beany or reaching out to touch her hand, when Della screamed above the din, "But what does it *mean!* I mean, does that mean God knew her little girl was going to choke? And if she was going to choke and He wanted Beany to save her, then why have her choke at *all?*"

For a moment no one had an answer, and they hated Della for asking the question. "But it's still a miracle, right?" asked Marina, who had said nothing since buying the drinks and toasting birth control pills. "Of course it is," and "Oh yes, I think so," and "A child was saved; that's all that matters," all the women chimed at once.

"My gosh, look at the time," said Salina. "We'll miss Freddie Fender."

"Let's have one more," said Marina. "We'll only miss the first band and we can see The Latin Express anytime down at The Four Queens."

Ruby got up from her stool behind the bar and began mixing fresh drinks.

"Well, I know *I* have to go," said Michelle, "before the kids start walking the three miles down here to get their own sodas."

The women told Michelle good-bye, then turned to each other asking who had the next miracle.

"Well," said Marina, "it didn't happen to me, but I read in the newspaper just the other day that a woman was trapped in her car for hours after it went off the highway. It happened somewhere back east. And it was real cold. And where her car went off the road was where no one would stop. And the road wasn't traveled much. And do you know what happened next?"

The women shook their heads, even Della, because of course they did not know what happened next.

"A man ran out of gas right there where the woman's car had gone off the road. And when he got out of the car he could hear her moaning. And so he walked to where he heard the moaning and saved her life. And I think that was a miracle."

The women nodded all together again. "Oh yes, amazing," and "Isn't that something," and "Gracias a Dios." The women were very impressed with this miracle even though it hadn't happened to anyone they knew.

"Well, the idiot had to run out of gas somewhere," said Della without looking up.

"Cabrona Della, do you have a stone in your chest instead of a heart?" said Dolores with her eyes narrowed.

"I just know that only men are stupid enough to run out of gas on a deserted road," Della shot back.

"What's that got to do with anything? And besides, it didn't have to be *that* deserted road, at *that* particular spot now, did it?" said Salina as she put her hand on her hip.

"You just don't understand coincidence. None of you. These are coincidences that turn out doing something good for somebody. That's all." Della's jaw clamped down.

It was a good thing Della had known these women all her life or she might have been called some names she wouldn't be able to forgive. Each of them had something to say about Della's disbelief, and they all said it at once. "What about the hand?" said Dolores. "It didn't have to be *that* road," said Marina. "We never knew who brought the food," said Hortencia. "The TV only worked long enough . . ."

Della put up her hands to fend off the assaults, then screamed louder than all of the women, "What about when the miracle means you die?"

The women looked at Della as if she had suddenly begun to speak in tongues.

"Della," said Dolores with exasperation, "what the hell are you talking about?"

"I'm talking about what about when the woman in the car doesn't get saved because some fool runs out of gas, and she just dies? Isn't that a coincidence, too, that nothing happened to save her? It's simple. Sometimes you make it through something and sometimes you don't. Look at the stuff that people should have made it through and they didn't. Is that a reverse miracle? And what's so goddamned great about living, anyway? You get told all this stuff about how wonderful the kingdom of God is, but nobody's in a hurry to see it, are they? If it's so goddamned wonderful, how come we all don't sit around praying to die as soon as possible? If all that shit is true, we ought to feel sorry for people who live through accidents and be happy for those who don't!" Della slammed her fist on the bar.

No one said a word until Hortencia waved an arm and said, "Bueno, otro trago para todos. I'm buying." Then everything was quiet again. Ruby got up to get the drinks, but before she could scoop ice into the first glass the phone rang. All of the women jumped because the quiet had filled the room to overflowing.

Ruby reached for the receiver, and smiled at the women as she did. "This is one time I can tell whoever it is that her husband really *isn't* here." No one laughed.

"El Nido Bar," said Ruby into the receiver. She listened for a moment. "Michelle?" Ruby put her hand over the mouthpiece and turned to the women, mouthing Michelle's name. "Wait, wait, slow down. Now, what happened to Jesse?" The women at the bar raised their heads, all of them looking at Ruby, trying to read her face. They all knew that Jesse was Michelle's youngest son, perhaps three years old now. Women in El Nido were raised to believe that all the children of their town belonged to everyone. It was common for women to wipe the noses of other women's children, scold them if the mother missed a trespass, or comfort them if they happened to be the one closest. Anything that had to do with the children of El Nido was the business of all. And now these women were watching the face of Ruby, holding their breath.

"You're kidding," said Ruby into the phone.

"What?!" clamored the women. Ruby put up her hand to keep them quiet. "Yes, yes, Beany's still here. Yes, I'll tell her. Yes, I'll tell them all. Yes, they're all still here. Yes, honey, now don't cry anymore."

The women were ready to jump the bar. Ruby gave them a smile to calm them and watched the breath they had been holding flow from their chests. "Yes," said Ruby, "I know. I'll tell them right now."

Ruby hung up the phone. "That was Michelle."

"Goddammit, Ruby, we *know* that. What happened?" Dolores wanted to hit her.

"Jessie. He was trying to swallow a piece of meat. They'd had dinner and Michelle hadn't cleared the food away yet. Jessie went back to the table when no one was looking and took a piece of meat. He was blue when Michelle found him. She did the Heimlich maneuver and it worked. She was crying because it scared her so badly and she was so happy it worked. She said if she hadn't forgotten the sodas, hadn't come in here tonight, hadn't waited to hear Beany's miracle, she wouldn't have known how to do the Heimlich maneuver."

Beany made the sign of the cross as thick rivulets of mascara ran down her cheeks. Salina and Marina hugged each other. All the women began hugging each other exclaiming, "Ay Dios, Madre," and "Gracias a Dios," and "Can you believe it?" Then the women looked at Della. Her face was buried in her hands and Dolores put an arm around her heaving shoulders.

Dolores held on to Della, letting her cry while the other women reached out to pat a shoulder, stroke an arm, touch her hair, or smooth away a rumple in her clothing.

"Can we keep just this one miracle, Della? Just this once," Dolores said gently into Della's hair.

With her hands still in front of her face, Della nodded her head. "Yes," she said through the lace of her fingers. "Oh, yes."

DAY AH DALLAS
MARE TOES

Luna Calderón

To Phil with love

MY NAME IS RÍO. KIDS ALWAYS SAY, "LIKE THE RIO GRAND?" AND
then crack up. I don't get what's so funny about that. Río, like Río J.
Olivares. That's it.

When I was born, my name was Río Jefferson. That sounds weird
but that's the name my mom gave me. Someday when I meet her, I'll
ask her why she named me Río. I don't know where the Jefferson came
from, 'cause she's Mexican, my bio logic mom is. My birth certificate
says, Father's name: unknown, Mother's name: Marta Pérez, Baby's
name: Río Jefferson. So when my dad adopted me, I got his last name.
Now my name is Río Jefferson Olivares.

Uncle Jeff is the white guy whose picture Daddy keeps on the mantle. I made up this story about him. It's not for real, but I like it. It's that
my bio logic mom used to know Uncle Jeff, and that he was my blood
father. Maybe Jeff is short for Jefferson. I keep thinking that Uncle Jeff
and me have to be blood related. Ever since I was little, like before
kindergarten, I heard whispering like wind in my ear. I finally figured

175

out it was Uncle Jeff. See, when I'd be falling asleep at night, I'd see his face smiling and floating around. I've had zillions of dreams about him. He tells me stories and funny things, like you're so cute, and let's eat chocolate. Also sometimes serious things. Like what to do when I have a problem. It's like my very own TV show.

There was the time when Doug Nelson kept sitting behind me in reading group and pulling my pony tail. I hate when people mess with my hair, so I was thinking about how to get him back. Then, in my dream that night, Uncle Jeff showed up and said, "Río, sweetie, Doug likes you. That's why he's acting like that." I listened to Uncle Jeff. Didn't do anything to Doug. He was right. On Valentimes, Doug Nelson put a big chocolate heart in my Valentimes box. He didn't give one to anybody else. I kept staring at him remembering what Uncle Jeff had said. He kept looking at his shoes. Then I stopped looking at him and just ate my chocolate heart. It was the good kind—no junk in the middle.

Next week I have an oral presentation for social studies. It's pretty much like show-and-tell, except we're too old to call it that. Miss Wilson said that we had to build an altar for a deceased relative because it's Día de los Muertos next week. 'Cept she said "Day Ah Dallas Mare Toes." Cici Ramírez and I cracked up, but not loud. We both pretend like we don't speak Spanish. But we do, and the way Miss Wilson said it was hecka stupid. When I got home, I saw Uncle Jeff on the mantle. I knew I had to make an altar for him. The next day I told Miss Wilson I didn't have any blood relatives. Told her I was choosing Uncle Jeff.

"Oh yes, well you have an alternative family," she said. "It's OK to bend the rules." I don't like social studies. I don't like Miss Wilson that much. I don't get it why she's so into Day Ah Dallas Mare Toes. She's not Mexican or Latin or nothing, I mean anything. When she was talking about it, the other kids in my class were rolling their eyes and going, "Ooooh, I don't want to give food to a dead person, that's weird." I rolled my eyes too, just so they wouldn't think I'm strange, but I know about this stuff.

Aunty T, that's my Daddy's best friend, he calls her his sister. She takes me to a Día de los Muertos thing every year. There's music and

Aztec dancing and a lot of altars. Some of them are cool. I asked Aunty T what the altars were for. To honor and respect the dead, she said. You put up pictures of dead people. Next to 'em you put flowers, their favorite food, stuff like that. She has an altar at her house with a lot of dead people. Uncle Jeff is one of them. One day I told her that I talked to him. She said she did too, like it was no big deal.

"We're not using a Ouija board. Are we doing it wrong?"

"Nah," she shook her head, "there's a lot of ways to communicate with those on the other side." That's what she calls dead people.

"I'm supposed to make an altar for Día de los Muertos. It's for Miss Wilson."

"What a great idea!" She was all excited.

"I don't like Miss Wilson."

"Sometimes people we don't like have good ideas."

I told her I didn't know anything about Uncle Jeff. Didn't know what to put on his altar. She told me a bunch of stuff. He was from Canada. The priests sent him here to the States. Uncle Jeff was a priest and so was Daddy. I wanted to know were they priests together? They weren't. They met after they left the priesthood. They left it 'cause they wanted to be openly gay.

"Couldn't they be openly gay priests?" I asked Aunty T.

"That's a whole other story," she said and never told me why.

Aunty T couldn't finish the story 'cause she had an appointment to get her nails done. I interrupted Dad from his reading even though I'm not supposed to. I knew he wouldn't care 'cause I needed to ask about homework. After Uncle Jeff decided to be openly gay, he went to social work school, and that's where he met Daddy and Aunty T. During that time, Daddy and Uncle Jeff were best friends. They lived together for a year. Uncle Jeff loved to clean and he was really nice, but after a while he got on Daddy's nerves.

"Why don't you move out from me? I get on your nerves practically every day," I wanted to know.

"This is different, I'm your father." Daddy's eyes got all big like the time I asked him if adopted fathers love their kids as much as blood fathers.

I asked him if I could have some ice cream. He said yes. We didn't talk about it anymore.

Later I asked Aunty T why Uncle Jeff got on Daddy's nerves. She looked kind of embarrassed. "It's no use keeping secrets." She told me the rest.

Uncle Jeff was in love with my Daddy. Same way Daddy loves his boyfriend John, and Doug Nelson loves me. But Daddy wasn't in love with Uncle Jeff. Just like I'm not in love with Doug. The difference is that Daddy liked Uncle Jeff like a friend. I don't like Doug like anything. I asked Aunty T if Uncle Jeff ever found another boyfriend. He didn't. He was sad about that. He wanted a boyfriend that looked like James Dean. He was always going on diets to lose weight so he could look better. It was hard 'cause he liked food a lot. Especially peanut butter and chocolate. Aunty T said Uncle Jeff was one of the nicest people she had ever met. She told me that one day he was standing on the street and he met this guy named Stephen. Stephen didn't have a place to live, 'cause he had run away from his mom in New Jersey. Uncle Jeff told him to come and stay at his house. Aunty T said she and Daddy were really mad at Uncle Jeff. They told him he was too nice. He could put himself in danger by inviting strangers to his house. But he didn't care. He did it anyway. Stephen got a job at a pizza place and slept on the couch. Until Uncle Jeff died.

Jeffery Robert De Angelo, that was his full name. He got run over by a car. On a Saturday. After breakfast. He had come over for pancakes with Aunty T and Daddy, then he went to buy a bed. A blue car hit him. He was crossing the street to get to the mattress store. Aunty T got tears in her eyes when she was telling me that part. I kind of felt like crying too. There was a big memorial service. I've never been to one. It's when they say nice things about the dead person right after they die. The room was really full. A lot of people came from Uncle Jeff's job. The ones that got there late had to stand up. For two hours, people said nice things about Uncle Jeff. Aunty T said Uncle Jeff was probably thrilled about that, where ever he was.

Stephen-the-pizza-guy didn't stand up to say anything, but the memorial service and the burial couldn't have happened without him.

He was the one who paid for it. Everybody was really worried about where the money was coming from. You need a lot of stuff when someone dies. A casket, a grave, food for the party. Stuff like that. Morticia was charging $8,000 even and nobody had that much money. Everyone was worried. Then, all of a sudden Stephen-the-pizza-guy walked out of Uncle Jeff's kitchen with a garbage bag that he kept in the freezer. It had $8,219 in it. He paid the bills and only had $219 left. After that, he took a bus to LA. Aunty T said no one ever heard from Stephen-the-pizza-guy again.

I started my altar. I'm using the Thanksgiving table cloth. Daddy said I could. He even gave me some stuff to put on it. A red toothbrush, some toothpaste, and Irish Spring soap because Uncle Jeff brushed his teeth and washed his face like twenty times a day. I got a bag of Reece's Peanut Butter Cups, a postcard of James Dean and a little sticker of a Canada flag. Daddy's letting me take the picture from the mantle to school on November first, the day of the oral report. Aunty T gave me a pack of Marlboro Cigarettes. She said Uncle Jeff smoked like a chimney. Everybody used to say it wasn't good for him. But she's glad he smoked. He really loved his cigarettes. Anyway, it didn't make any difference 'cause he got hit by a car. When it's your time, it's your time.

I'm also making Uncle Jeff a card. On the outside it has a big red heart. On the inside it says "Dear Uncle Jeff, Happy Dah Ah Dallas Mare Toes. Ha-ha. I love you very Much. Love Río." My handwriting isn't so good, but I'm sure Uncle Jeff can read it. Dead people know everything anyways.

CONTRIBUTORS

Kathleen Alcalá is the author of a short story collection, *Mrs. Vargas and the Dead Naturalist* (Calyx), and three novels set in nineteenth-century Mexico: *Spirits of the Ordinary, The Flower in the Skull,* and *Treasures in Heaven* (Chronicle, Harvest/Harcourt Brace). Her work has received the Pacific Northwest Booksellers Award, the Governor's Writers Award, and the Western States Book Award for Fiction. She is a cofounder of and contributing editor to *The Raven Chronicles.*

Luna Calderón is a hybrid Latina—she was born in Brazil and raised in Mexico and the United States. She received her M.F.A. from Mills College. She is currently editing an anthology on women writers of color and completing her first novel. Calderón is a full-time psychotherapist who works with youth. She lives in Berkeley with her partner and their two cats.

Brandt Jesús Cooper submitted "A New Night of Long Knives" to this collection and then disappeared. The editors hope to hear from him upon publication of the book.

Rubén Degollado's work has appeared in *Beloit Fiction Journal, Bilingual Review/Revista Bilingüe, Gulf Coast, Hayden's Ferry Review,* and *Image.* He just completed a novel titled "Throw" and is currently at work on "Host," a collection of interrelated short stories about the Izquierdo family. Originally from McAllen, Texas, he is an ESL and bilingual education teacher in Oregon and a graduate student at Lewis & Clark College.

Elena Díaz Björkquist is a retired educator who taught California students at elementary and high school levels and at a state university. Currently she is an educational consultant and writer living in Tucson. She writes stories about Morenci, Arizona, where she was born. Her book of poetry, *Rediscovering My Spirit,* was published in 1991, and her book of short stories, *Suffer Smoke,* was published in 1996. A new collection of young adult stories called *Water from the Moon* is due out in 2001. "Inocente's Getaway" is also in her new manuscript, "Albóndiga Soup." Ms. Björkquist was recently funded by the Arizona Humanities Council to do an oral history of the Chicanos in Morenci during the Depression and World War II.

Guadalupe García Montaño is a native of Los Angeles and a graduate of University of California at Los Angeles and the University of Texas at El Paso. She is currently an instructor of English at East Los Angeles College.

Lucrecia Guerrero grew up in Nogales, Arizona, on the Mexican American border and has also lived in Ohio and Mexico. Her writing reflects these three regions. Guerrero now writes and teaches in Dayton, Ohio, and is interested in promoting the Latina/o voice through the arts as a writer and board member of the Ohio Latin Artists Association. "Hotel Arco Iris" appears in Guerrero's debut collection of short stories, *Chasing Shadows* (Chronicle Books, 2000). Other individual stories have appeared in journals including *ByLine* and a special Latino edition of the *Colorado Review.* She is a Pushcart Prize nominee and a recipient of the Montgomery Culture Arts Fellowship. She is currently writing a novel.

Stephen D. Gutiérrez is the winner of the 1996 Charles H. and N. Mildred Nilon Excellence in Minority Fiction Award for his book *ELEMENTS*. He has published stories and essays in *Fiction International, Puerto Del Sol, Riversedge, Santa Monica Review*, and *ZYZZYVA*. His work has also appeared in the anthology *Latino Heretics*. "Cantinflas" is part of a work-in-progress blending social history, current politics, and short stories. He teaches at California State University, Hayward.

Gary G. Hernández has many painful obsessions, one of which is writing. The others include ultra-marathon running, adjunct teaching at Citrus Community College in California, working full-time at a very large oil company, and pursuing yet another degree (M.S. in technical writing at Utah State University). His writing accomplishments include second place in the *Las Vegas CityLife* 2000 short fiction contest and placement in this very anthology. Hernández is an avid lover of tales of horror and the supernatural. He is especially fond of horror tales infused with religious mythos such as those in the Faustian and Lilith traditions.

Kelley Jácquez wrote her first short story in her senior year of college at the behest of one of her college professors. To her surprise, the professor submitted the story to a small literary magazine and it was published. "It scared the hell out of me," said Jácquez, "because I realized I'd have to do it again." She has since published ten short stories in literary magazines and anthologies, and six of her stories have been recorded for radio for a listening audience of three million. She is currently finishing a collection of short stories set in New Mexico titled "Ordinary Madness."

Rob Johnson is an assistant professor of English at The University of Texas-Pan American in Edinburg, Texas. He has published essays on Southwest and border writers such as David Rice, Kathleen Alcalá, María Cristina Mena, and Katherine Anne Porter. He recently published an article titled "William S. Burroughs: South Texas Farmer, Junky, and Queer" in *Southwestern American Literature*, and he is at work on a full-length biographical study of Burroughs's south Texas adventures titled "Tiger in the Valley."

A pocha raised between San Antonio, Texas, and Dillingham, Alaska, **Jacquie Moody** works for the San Antonio AIDS Foundation by day. By night she is an aspiring poet and fiction writer trying to save up enough money for an M.F.A.

Daniel A. Olivas is the author of *The Courtship of María Rivera Peña: A Novella* (Silver Lake Publishing, 2000). His fiction and poetry have appeared in *Exquisite Corpse, THEMA, The Pacific Review, Red River Review, Riversedge,* and *Web del Sol,* among many others. The author's work is featured in several anthologies including *Love to Mamá: A Tribute to Mothers,* edited by Pat Mora (Lee & Low Books, 2001), and *Nemeton: A Fables Anthology,* edited by Megan Powell (Silver Lake Publishing, 2000). He received his B.A. in English literature from Stanford University and law degree from the University of California at Los Angeles. The author practices law with the California Department of Justice, specializing in land use and environmental enforcement. He makes his home with his wife and son in the San Fernando Valley.

Torie Olson's short fiction has been nominated for a Pushcart Prize and published in *Calyx, Literal Latté, Prairie Schooner,* and other literary magazines. "Tear Out My Heart" is part of her linked collection of stories titled "Crazy Ladies."

Karleen Pendleton Jiménez is a writer and teacher. She is a member of Lengua Latina, a writing group for Latinas in Toronto. She has published several short stories in erotic anthologies and has just recently published the children's book *Are You a Boy or a Girl?,* which was named as a finalist for a 2001 Lambda Literary Award.

Stephanie R. Reyes lives in Austin and, last we heard, is trying to decide whether she should attend law school or pursue an M.F.A. in creative writing. "Bad Debts and Vindictive Women" is her first published story.

David Rice was born in Weslaco, Texas, in 1964. He is the author of *Give the Pig a Chance* (Bilingual Press, 1994) and *Crazy Loco* (Dial Books, 2001), two collections of short stories set in the valley of south

Texas. As the writer-in-residence for the Llano Grande Center for Research and Development in Edcouch, Texas, Rice teaches creative writing and mentors high school students. Rice also writes and directs plays and short films.

René Saldaña, Jr., is a Ph.D. candidate in English and creative writing at Georgia State University in Atlanta. His poetry and stories have appeared or are forthcoming in *Texas Short Stories II*, *Maelstrom*, *African Voices*, *Southwestern American Literature*, *Mesquite Review*, and *Bathtub Gin*, among others. His first novel, *The Jumping Tree*, was published by Random House/Delacorte in 2001.

Carmen Tafolla is the author most recently of *Sonnets and Salsa!*, a collection of poems published by Wings Press. Her previous books include the children's book *Baby Coyote and the Old Woman/El Coyotito y la Viejita* (Wings Press, 2000) and *Sonnets to Human Beings* (McGraw-Hill, 1989), which features Tafolla's short stories and poems. Tafolla is a popular performer of her work; she lives in San Antonio, Texas.

Elva Treviño Hart's first book, *Barefoot Heart: Stories of a Migrant Child*, a memoir, won the American Book Award, the American Library Association's Alex Award, and the Violet Crown. Interviews with Treviño Hart have been broadcast nationally on C-SPAN's "Book TV" and the Diane Rehm show on National Public Radio. "Beyond Eternity" is included in her short-story collection "The Maids of San Miguel." She lives in Charlottesville, Virginia, and is working on a novel set in south Texas and a Spanish translation of *Barefoot Heart*.